Goosebumps

WELCOME TO DEAD HOUSE

I could feel myself start to choke. I couldn't breathe. I couldn't move. I opened my mouth to call out to Josh, but no sound came out.

Josh? Where was he?

I looked down the rows of gravestones but couldn't see his light.

Ray floated up a little higher. He hovered over me, choking me somehow, blinding me, suffocating me.

I'm dead, I thought. Dead.

Now I'm dead, too.

When Amanda and Josh move to Dark Falls they're not too sure about their new neighbourhood. There's something odd about the kids who live there. They're friendly, all right, maybe a little *too* friendly. In fact, they want to be friends . . . *forever.*

D1380123

Also in this series:

Goosebumps

WELCOME TO DEAD HOUSE

R.L. STINE

Hippo

Scholastic Children's Books,
Commonwealth House, 1–19 New Oxford Street, London WC1A 1NU, UK
a division of Scholastic Ltd
London ~ New York ~ Toronto ~ Sydney ~ Auckland
Mexico City ~ New Delhi ~ Hong Kong

First published in the USA by Scholastic Inc., 1992
First published in the UK by Scholastic Ltd, 1993

Copyright © Parachute Press, Inc., 1992
GOOSEBUMPS is a trademark of Parachute Press, Inc.

ISBN: 0 439 01198 1

Printed and bound by Cox & Wyman Ltd., Reading, Berks

10 9 8 7 6 5 4 3 2 1

Josh and I hated our new house.

Okay, it was big. It looked like a mansion compared to our old house. It was a tall redbrick house with a sloping black roof and rows of windows framed by black shutters.

It's so dark, I thought, studying it from the street. The whole house was covered in darkness, as if it were hiding in the shadows of the gnarled, old trees that bent over it.

It was the middle of July, but dead brown leaves blanketed the front garden. Our trainers crunched over them as we trudged up the gravel drive.

Tall weeds poked up everywhere through the dead leaves. Thick clumps of weeds had completely overgrown an old flower bed beside the front porch.

This house is creepy, I thought unhappily.

Josh must have been thinking the same thing. Looking up at the old house, we both groaned loudly.

1

Mr Dawes, the friendly young man from the local estate agents, stopped near the front path and turned round.

"Everything okay?" he asked, staring first at Josh, then at me, with his crinkly blue eyes.

"Josh and Amanda aren't happy about moving," Dad explained, tucking his shirt-tail in. Dad is a little overweight, and his shirts always seem to be coming untucked.

"It's hard for the kids," my mother added, smiling at Mr Dawes, her hands shoved into her jeans pockets as she continued up to the front door. "You know. Leaving all their friends behind. Moving to a strange new place."

"Strange is right," Josh said, shaking his head. "This house is gross."

Mr Dawes chuckled. "It's an old house, that's for sure," he said, patting Josh on the shoulder.

"It just needs some work, Josh," Dad said, smiling at Mr Dawes. "No one has lived in it for a while, so it'll take some doing up."

"Look how big it is," Mum added, smoothing back her straight black hair and smiling at Josh. "We'll have room for a study and maybe a TV room, too. You'd like that — wouldn't you, Amanda?"

I shrugged. A cold breeze made me shiver. It was actually a beautiful, hot summer's day. But the closer we got to the house, the colder I felt.

I supposed it was because of all the tall, old trees.

I was wearing white tennis shorts and a sleeveless T-shirt. It had been hot in the car. But now I was freezing. Maybe it'll be warmer in the house, I thought.

"How old are they?" Mr Dawes asked Mum, stepping onto the front porch.

"Amanda is twelve," Mum answered. "And Josh was eleven last month."

"They look so much alike," Mr Dawes told Mum.

I couldn't decide if that was a compliment or not. I suppose it's true. Josh and I are both tall and thin and have curly brown hair like Dad's, and dark brown eyes. Everyone says we have "serious" faces.

"I really want to go home," Josh said, his voice cracking. "I hate this place."

My brother is the most impatient kid in the world. And when he makes up his mind about something, that's it. He's a little spoiled. At least, I think so. Whenever he makes a big fuss about something, he usually gets his way.

We may look alike, but we're really not that similar. I'm a lot more patient than Josh is. A lot more sensible. Probably because I'm older and because I'm a girl.

Josh was holding Dad's hand and trying to

pull him back to the car. "Let's go. Come on, Dad. Let's go."

I knew this was one time Josh wouldn't get his own way. We were moving to this house. No doubt about it. After all, the house was absolutely free. A great-uncle of Dad's, a man we didn't even know, had died and left the house to Dad in his will.

I'll never forget the look on Dad's face when he got the letter from the lawyer. He let out a loud whoop and began dancing around the living room. Josh and I thought he'd flipped or something.

"My Great-Uncle Charles has left us a house in his will," Dad explained, reading and rereading the letter. "It's in a town called Dark Falls."

"Huh?" Josh and I cried. "Where's Dark Falls?"

Dad shrugged.

"I don't remember your Uncle Charles," Mum said, moving behind Dad to read the letter over his shoulder.

"Neither do I," admitted Dad. "But he must've been a great guy! Wow! This sounds like an incredible house!" He grabbed Mum's hands and began dancing happily with her across the living room.

Dad certainly was excited. He'd been looking for an excuse to give up his boring office job and devote all of his time to his writing career. This

4

house — absolutely free — would be just the excuse he needed.

And now, a week later, here we were in Dark Falls, a four-hour drive from our home, seeing our new house for the first time. We hadn't even gone inside, and Josh was trying to drag Dad back to the car.

"Josh — stop pulling me," Dad snapped impatiently, trying to tug his hand out of Josh's grasp.

Dad glanced helplessly at Mr Dawes. I could see that he was embarrassed by how Josh was carrying on. I decided maybe I could help.

"Let's go, Josh," I said quietly, grabbing Josh by the shoulder. "We promised we'd give Dark Falls a chance — remember?"

"I already gave it a chance," Josh whined, not letting go of Dad's hand. "This house is old and ugly and I hate it."

"You haven't even gone inside," Dad said angrily.

"Yes. Let's go in," Mr Dawes urged, staring at Josh.

"I'm staying outside," Josh insisted.

He can be really stubborn sometimes. I felt just as unhappy as Josh looking at this dark, old house. But I'd never carry on the way Josh was.

"Josh, don't you want to choose your own room?" Mum asked.

"No," Josh muttered.

5

He and I both glanced up to the first floor. There were two large bay windows side by side up there. They looked like two dark eyes staring back at us.

"How long have you lived in your present house?" Mr Dawes asked Dad.

Dad had to think for a second. "About fourteen years," he answered. "The kids have lived there all their lives."

"Moving is always hard," Mr Dawes said sympathetically, turning his gaze on me. "You know, Amanda, I moved here to Dark Falls just a few months ago. I didn't like it much either, at first. But now I wouldn't live anywhere else." He winked at me. He had a cute dimple in his chin when he smiled. "Let's go inside. It's really quite nice. You'll be surprised."

All of us followed Mr Dawes, except Josh. "Are there other kids in this street?" Josh demanded. He made it sound more like a challenge than a question.

Mr Dawes nodded. "The school's just two blocks away," he said, pointing up the street.

"See?" Mum quickly cut in. "A short walk to school. No more long bus rides every morning."

"I *liked* the bus," Josh insisted.

His mind was made up. He wasn't going to give my parents a chance, even though we'd both promised to be open-minded about this move.

I don't know what Josh thought he had to gain

by being such a pain. I mean, Dad already had plenty to worry about. For one thing, he hadn't been able to sell our old house yet.

I didn't like the idea of moving. But I knew that inheriting this big house was a great opportunity for us. We were so cramped in our little house. And once Dad managed to sell the old place, we wouldn't have to worry about money at all any more.

Josh should at least give it a chance. That's what I thought.

Suddenly, from our car at the foot of the drive, we heard Petey barking and howling and making a fuss.

Petey is our dog, a white, curly-haired terrier, cute as a button, and usually well-behaved. He never minded being left in the car. But now he was yowling and yapping at full volume and scratching at the car window, desperate to get out.

"Petey — quiet! Quiet!" I shouted. Petey usually listened to me.

But not this time.

"I'm going to let him out!" Josh declared, and took off down the drive, towards the car.

"No. Wait —" Dad called.

But I don't think Josh could hear him over Petey's wails.

"Might as well let the dog explore," Mr Dawes said. "It's going to be his house, too."

7

A few seconds later, Petey came charging across the lawn, kicking up brown leaves, yipping excitedly as he ran up to us. He jumped on all of us as if he hadn't seen us in weeks and then, to our surprise, he started growling menacingly and barking at Mr Dawes.

"Petey — stop!" Mum yelled.

"He's never done this," Dad said apologetically. "Really. He's usually very friendly."

"He probably smells something on me. Another dog, maybe," Mr Dawes said, loosening his striped tie, looking warily at our growling dog.

Finally, Josh grabbed Petey around the middle and lifted him away from Mr Dawes. "Stop it, Petey," Josh scolded, holding the dog up close to his face so that they were nose-to-nose. "Mr Dawes is our friend."

Petey whimpered and licked Josh's face. After a while, Josh put him back down on the ground. Petey looked up at Mr Dawes, then at me, then decided to go sniffing around the garden, letting his nose lead the way.

"Let's go inside," Mr Dawes urged, moving a hand through his short blond hair. He unlocked the front door and pushed it open.

Mr Dawes held the screen door open for us. I started to follow my parents into the house.

"I'll stay out here with Petey," Josh insisted from the path.

Dad started to protest, but changed his mind.

8

"Okay. Fine," he said, sighing and shaking his head. "I'm not going to argue with you. Don't come in. You can *live* outside if you want." He sounded really exasperated.

"I want to stay with Petey," Josh said again, watching Petey nose his way through the dead flower bed.

Mr Dawes followed us into the hall, gently closing the screen door behind him, giving Josh a final glance. "He'll be fine," he said softly, smiling at Mum.

"He can be so stubborn sometimes," Mum said apologetically. She peeped into the living room. "I'm really sorry about Petey. I don't know what got into him."

"No problem. Let's start in the living room," Mr Dawes said, leading the way. "I think you'll be pleasantly surprised by how spacious it is. Of course, it needs work."

He took us on a tour of every room in the house. I was beginning to get excited. The house was pretty cool really. There were so many rooms and so many cupboards. And my room was huge and had its own bathroom and an old-fashioned window seat where I could sit at the window and look down the street.

I wished Josh had come inside with us. If he could see how great the house was inside, I knew he'd start to cheer up.

I couldn't believe how many rooms there were.

Even a finished attic filled with old furniture and stacks of old, mysterious boxes we could explore.

We must have been inside for at least half an hour. I didn't really keep track of time. I think all three of us were feeling cheered up.

"Well, I think I've shown you everything," Mr Dawes said, glancing at his watch. He led the way to the front door.

"Wait — I want to take one more look at my room," I told them excitedly. I started up the stairs, taking them two at a time. "I'll be down in a second."

"Hurry, dear. I'm sure Mr Dawes has other appointments," Mum called after me.

I reached the first-floor landing and hurried down the narrow hall and into my new room. "Wow!" I said aloud, and the word echoed faintly against the empty walls.

It was so big. And I loved the bay window with the window seat. I walked over to it and peered out. Through the trees, I could see our car in the drive and, beyond it, a house that looked a lot like ours across the street.

I'm going to put my bed against that wall opposite the window, I thought happily. And my desk can go over there. I'll have room for a computer now!

I took one more look at my wardrobe, a long, walk-in wardrobe with a light in the ceiling, and

10

wide shelves against the back wall.

I was heading for the door, thinking about which of my posters I wanted to bring with me, when I saw the boy.

He stood in the doorway for just a second. And then he turned and disappeared down the hall.

"Josh?" I cried. "Hey — come and look!"

With a shock, I realized it wasn't Josh.

For one thing, the boy had blond hair.

"Hey!" I called and ran to the landing, stopping just outside my bedroom door, looking both ways. "Who's here?"

But the long hall was empty. All the doors were closed.

"Whoa, Amanda," I said aloud.

Was I seeing things?

Mum and Dad were calling from downstairs. I took one last look down the dark corridor, then hurried to rejoin them.

"Hey, Mr Dawes," I called as I ran down the stairs, "is this house haunted?"

He chuckled. The question seemed to strike him as funny. "No. Sorry," he said, looking at me with those crinkly blue eyes. "No ghost included. A lot of old houses around here are said to be haunted. But I'm afraid this isn't one of them."

"I — I thought I saw something," I said, feeling a little foolish.

"Probably just shadows," Mum said. "With all the trees, this house is so dark."

11

"Why don't you run outside and tell Josh about the house," Dad suggested, tucking in the front of his shirt. "Your mum and I have some things to talk over with Mr Dawes."

"Yes, master," I said with a little bow, and obediently ran out to tell Josh all about what he had missed. "Hey, Josh," I called, eagerly searching in the garden. "Josh?"

My heart sank.

Josh and Petey had gone.

"Josh! Josh!"

First I called Josh. Then I called Petey. But there was no sign of either of them.

I ran down to the bottom of the drive and peered into the car, but they weren't there. Mum and Dad were still inside talking to Mr Dawes. I looked along the street in both directions, but there was no sign of them.

"Josh! Hey, Josh!"

Finally, Mum and Dad came hurrying out of the front door, looking alarmed. I suppose they'd heard my shouts. "I can't find Josh or Petey!" I yelled up to them from the street.

"Maybe they're out the back," Dad shouted down to me.

I headed up the drive, kicking away dead leaves as I ran. It was sunny down on the street, but as soon as I entered our garden, I was back in the shade, and it was immediately cool again.

"Hey, Josh! Josh — where are you?"

Why did I feel so scared? It was perfectly natural for Josh to wander off. He did it all the time.

I ran full speed along the side of the house. Tall trees leaned over the house on this side, blocking out nearly all of the sunlight.

The back garden was bigger than I'd expected, a long rectangle that sloped gradually down to a wooden fence at the back. Just like the front, this garden was a mass of tall weeds, poking up through a thick covering of brown leaves. A stone birdbath had toppled onto its side. Beyond it, I could see the side of the garage, a dark, brick building that matched the house.

"Hey — Josh!"

He wasn't back here. I stopped and searched the ground for footprints or a sign that he had run through the thick leaves.

"Well?" Out of breath, Dad came jogging up to me.

"No sign of him," I said, surprised at how worried I felt.

"Did you check the car?" He sounded more angry than worried.

"Yes. It's the first place I looked." I gave the back garden a last quick search. "I can't believe Josh would just run off."

"I do," Dad said, rolling his eyes. "You know your brother when he doesn't get his own way.

14

Maybe he wants us to think he's run away from home." He frowned.

"Where is he?" Mum asked as we returned to the front of the house.

Dad and I both shrugged. "Maybe he made a friend and wandered off," Dad said. He raised a hand and scratched his curly brown hair. I could tell that he was starting to worry, too.

"We've *got* to find him," Mum said, gazing down to the street. "He doesn't know this neighbourhood at all. He probably wandered off and has got lost."

Mr Dawes locked the front door and stepped down off the porch, pocketing the keys. "He couldn't have got far," he said, giving Mum a reassuring smile. "Let's drive around the streets. I'm sure we'll find him."

Mum shook her head and glanced nervously at Dad. "I'll kill him," she muttered. Dad patted her on the shoulder.

Mr Dawes opened the boot of the small Honda, pulled off his dark blazer, and tossed it inside. Then he took out a wide-brimmed, black cowboy hat and put it on his head.

"Hey — that's quite a hat," Dad said, climbing into the front passenger seat.

"Keeps the sun away," Mr Dawes said, sliding behind the wheel and slamming the car door.

Mum and I got in the back. Glancing over at her, I saw that Mum was as worried as I was.

15

We headed down the street in silence, all four of us staring out of the car windows. The houses we passed all seemed old. Most of them were even bigger than our house. All of them seemed to be in better condition, nicely painted with neat, well-trimmed lawns.

I didn't see any people in the houses or gardens, and there was no one on the street.

It certainly is a *quiet* neighbourhood, I thought. And shady. The houses all seemed to be surrounded by tall, leafy trees. The front gardens we drove slowly past all seemed to be bathed in shade. The street was the only sunny place, a narrow gold ribbon that ran through the shadows on both sides.

Maybe that's why it's called Dark Falls, I thought.

"Where is that son of mine?" Dad asked, staring hard out of the windscreen.

"I'll kill him. I really will," Mum muttered. It wasn't the first time she had said that about Josh.

We had gone round the block twice. No sign of him.

Mr Dawes suggested we drive round the next few blocks, and Dad quickly agreed. "Hope I don't get lost. I'm new here, too," Mr Dawes said, turning a corner. "Hey, there's the school," he announced, pointing out of the window at a tall redbrick building. It looked very old-fashioned, with white columns on both sides of the double front doors. "Of course, it's closed now," Mr Dawes added.

My eyes searched the fenced-in playground behind the school. It was empty. No one there.

"Could Josh have walked this far?" Mum asked, her voice tight and higher than usual.

"Josh doesn't walk," Dad said, rolling his eyes. "He runs."

"We'll find him," Mr Dawes said confidently, tapping his fingers on the wheel as he steered.

We turned a corner onto another shady block. A street sign read "Cemetery Drive", and sure enough, a large cemetery rose up in front of us. Granite gravestones rolled along a low hill, which sloped down and then up again onto a large flat stretch, also marked with rows of low grave markers and monuments.

A few shrubs dotted the cemetery, but there weren't many trees. As we drove slowly past, the gravestones passing by in a blur on the left, I realized that this was the sunniest spot I had seen in the whole town.

"There's your son." Mr Dawes, pointing out of the window, stopped the car suddenly.

"Oh, thank goodness!" Mum exclaimed, leaning down to see out of the window on my side of the car.

Sure enough, there was Josh, running wildly along a crooked row of low, white gravestones.

17

"What's he doing *here*?" I asked, pushing open my car door.

I stepped down from the car, took a few steps onto the grass, and called to him. At first, he didn't react to my shouts. He seemed to be ducking and dodging through the tombstones. He would run in one direction, then cut to the side, then head in another direction.

Why was he doing that?

I took another few steps — and then stopped, gripped with fear.

I suddenly realized why Josh was darting and ducking like that, running so wildly through the tombstones. He was being chased.

Someone — or something — was after him.

Then, as I took a few reluctant steps towards Josh, watching him bend low, then change directions, his arms outstretched as he ran, I realized I had it completely wrong.

Josh wasn't being chased. Josh was *chasing*.

He was chasing after Petey.

Okay, okay. So sometimes my imagination runs away with me. Running through an old graveyard like this — even in bright daylight — it's only natural that a person might start to have weird thoughts.

I called to Josh again, and this time he heard me and turned round. He looked worried. "Amanda — come and help me!" he cried.

"Josh, what's the matter?" I ran as fast as I could to catch up with him, but he kept darting through the gravestones, moving from row to row.

"Help!"

"Josh — what's wrong?" I turned and saw

19

that Mum and Dad were right behind me.

"It's Petey," Josh explained, out of breath. "I can't get him to stop. I caught him once, but he pulled away from me."

"Petey! Petey!" Dad started calling the dog. But Petey was moving from stone to stone, sniffing each one, then running to the next.

"How did you get all the way over here?" Dad asked as he caught up with my brother.

"I had to follow Petey," Josh explained, still looking very worried. "He just took off. One second he was sniffing around that dead flower bed in our front garden. The next second, he just started to run. He wouldn't stop when I called. Wouldn't even look back. He kept running till he got here. I had to follow. I was afraid he'd get lost."

Josh stopped and gratefully let Dad take over the chase. "I don't know what that stupid dog's problem is," he said to me. "He's just *weird*."

It took Dad a few tries, but he finally managed to grab Petey and pick him up off the ground. Our little terrier gave a half-hearted yelp of protest, then allowed himself to be carried away.

We all trooped back to the car on the side of the road. Mr Dawes was waiting by the car. "Maybe you'd better get a leash for that dog," he said, looking very concerned.

"Petey's never been on a leash," Josh protested, wearily climbing into the back seat.

"Well, we might have to try one for a while," Dad said quietly. "Especially if he keeps running away." Dad tossed Petey into the back seat. The dog eagerly curled up in Josh's arms.

The rest of us piled into the car, and Mr Dawes drove us back to his office, a tiny, white, flat-roofed building at the end of a row of small offices. As we drove, I reached over and stroked the back of Petey's head.

Why did the dog run away like that? I wondered. Petey had never done that before.

I thought that Petey was also upset about our moving. After all, Petey had spent his whole life in our old house. He probably felt a lot like Josh and I did about having to pack up and move and never see the old neighbourhood again.

The new house, the new streets, and all the new smells must have freaked the poor dog out. Josh wanted to run away from the whole idea. And so did Petey.

Anyway, that was my theory.

Mr Dawes parked the car in front of his tiny office, shook Dad's hand, and gave him a business card. "You can drop by next week," he told Mum and Dad. "I'll have all the legal work done by then. After you sign the papers, you can move in at any time."

He pushed open the car door and, giving us all a final smile, prepared to climb out.

"Compton Dawes," Mum said, reading the

white business card over Dad's shoulder. "That's an unusual name. Is Compton an old family name?"

Mr Dawes shook his head. "No," he said, "I'm the only Compton in my family. I have no idea where the name comes from. No idea at all. Maybe my parents didn't know how to spell Charlie!"

Chuckling at his terrible joke, he climbed out of the car, lowered the wide black Stetson hat on his head, pulled his blazer from the boot, and disappeared into the small white building.

Dad climbed behind the wheel, moving the seat back to make room for his big stomach. Mum got in the front, and we started the long drive home. "I suppose you and Petey had quite an adventure today," Mum said to Josh, rolling up her window because Dad had turned on the air conditioner.

"I suppose so," Josh said without enthusiasm. Petey was sound asleep in his lap, snoring quietly.

"You're going to love your room," I told Josh. "The whole house is great. Really."

Josh stared at me thoughtfully, but didn't answer.

I poked him in the ribs with my elbow. "Say something. Did you hear what I said?"

But the weird, thoughtful look didn't fade from Josh's face.

The next couple of weeks seemed to crawl by. I walked around the house thinking about how I'd never see my room again, how I'd never eat breakfast in this kitchen again, how I'd never watch TV in the living room again. Morbid stuff like that.

I had this sick feeling when the removal men came one afternoon and delivered a tall stack of boxes. Time to pack up. It was really happening. Even though it was the middle of the afternoon, I went up to my room and flopped down on my bed. I didn't sleep or anything. I just stared at the ceiling for more than an hour, and all these wild, unconnected thoughts ran through my head, like a dream, only I was awake.

I wasn't the only one who was nervous about the move. Mum and Dad were snapping at each other over nothing at all. One morning they had a big row over whether the bacon was too crispy or not.

In a way, it was funny to see them being so childish. Josh was acting really sullen all the time. He hardly said a word to anyone. And Petey sulked, too. That stupid dog wouldn't even pick himself up and come over to me when I had some table scraps for him.

I suppose the hardest part about moving was saying goodbye to my friends. Carol and Amy were away at camp, so I had to write to them. But Kathy was home, and she was my oldest and best friend, and the hardest to say goodbye to.

I think some people were surprised that Kathy and I had stayed such good friends. For one thing, we look so different. I'm tall and thin and dark, and she's fair-skinned, with long blonde hair, and a little chubby. But we've been friends since nursery school, and best friends since the fourth grade.

When she came over the night before the move, we were both terribly awkward. "Kathy, you shouldn't be nervous," I told her. "You're not the one who's moving away forever."

"It's not as if you're moving to China or anything," she answered, chewing hard on her bubble gum. "Dark Falls is only four hours away, Amanda. We'll see each other a lot."

"Yeah, I suppose so," I said. But I didn't believe it. Four hours away was as bad as being in China, as far as I was concerned. "I suppose we can still talk on the phone," I said glumly.

She blew a small green bubble, then sucked it back into her mouth. "Yeah. Of course," she said, pretending to be enthusiastic. "You're lucky, you know. Moving out of this crummy neighbourhood to a big house."

"It's *not* a crummy neighbourhood," I insisted. I don't know why I was defending the neighbourhood. I never had before. One of our favourite pastimes was thinking of places where we'd rather be growing up.

"School won't be the same without you," she sighed, curling her legs under her on the chair. "Who's going to tell me the answers in maths?"

I laughed. "I always gave you the *wrong* answers."

"But it was the thought that counted," Kathy said. And then she groaned. "Ugh. Junior high. Is your new junior high part of the high school or part of the elementary school?"

I made a disgusted face. "Everything's in one building. It's a small town, remember? There's no separate high school. At least, I didn't see one."

"Bummer," she said.

Bummer was right.

We chatted for hours. Until Kathy's mum called and said it was time for her to come home.

Then we hugged. I had made up my mind that I wouldn't cry, but I could feel the big, hot tears forming in the corners of my eyes. And then they were running down my cheeks.

"I'm so miserable!" I wailed.

I had planned to be really controlled and mature. But Kathy was my best friend, after all, and what could I do?

We made a promise that we'd always be together on our birthdays — no matter what. We'd force our parents to make sure we didn't miss each other's birthdays.

And then we hugged again. And Kathy said,

"Don't worry. We'll see each other a lot. Really."
And she had tears in her eyes, too.

She turned and ran out of the door. The screen door slammed hard behind her. I stood there staring out into the darkness until Petey came scampering in, his toenails clicking across the linoleum, and started to lick my hand.

The next morning, moving day, was a rainy Saturday. Not a downpour. No thunder or lightning. But just enough rain and wind to make the long drive slow and unpleasant.

The sky seemed to get darker as we neared the new neighbourhood. The heavy trees bent low over the street. "Slow down, Jack," Mum warned shrilly. "The roads are really slippery."

But Dad was in a hurry to get to the house before the removal van did. "They'll just put the stuff anywhere if we're not there to supervise," he explained.

Josh, beside me in the back seat, was being a real pain, as usual. He kept complaining that he was thirsty. When that didn't get results, he started whining that he was starving. But we had all had a big breakfast, so that didn't get any reaction, either.

He just wanted attention, of course. I kept trying to cheer him up by telling him how great the house was inside and how big his room was. He still hadn't seen it.

26

But he didn't want to be cheered up. He started wrestling with Petey, getting the poor dog all worked up, until Dad had to shout at him to stop.

"Let's all try really hard not to get on each other's nerves," Mum suggested.

Dad laughed. "Good idea, dear."

"Don't make fun of me," she snapped.

They started to argue about who was more exhausted from all the packing. Petey stood up on his hind legs and started to howl at the back window.

"Can't you shut him up?" Mum screamed.

I pulled Petey down, but he struggled back and started howling again. "He's never done this before," I said.

"Just keep him quiet!" Mum insisted.

I pulled Petey down by his hind legs, and Josh started to howl. Mum turned round and gave him a dirty look. Josh didn't stop howling, though. He thought he was a riot.

Finally, Dad pulled the car up the drive of the new house. The tyres crunched over the wet gravel. Rain pounded on the roof.

"Home sweet home," Mum said. I couldn't tell if she was being sarcastic or not. I think she was just glad the long car journey was over.

"At least we beat the removal van," Dad said, glancing at his watch. Then his expression changed. "Hope they're not lost."

"It's pitch black out there," Josh complained.

Petey was jumping up and down in my lap, desperate to get out of the car. He was usually a good traveller. But once the car had stopped, he wanted to get out immediately.

I opened my car door and he leaped onto the drive with a splash and started to run in a wild zigzag across the front garden.

"At least *someone's* glad to be here," Josh said quietly.

Dad ran up to the porch and, fumbling with the unfamiliar keys, managed to get the front door open. Then he motioned for us to come into the house.

Mum and Josh ran up the path, eager to get in out of the rain. I closed the car door behind me and started to jog after them.

But something caught my eye. I stopped and looked up at the twin bay windows above the porch.

I held a hand over my eyebrows to shield my eyes and squinted through the rain.

Yes. I saw it.

A face. In the window on the left.

The boy.

The same boy was up there, staring down at me.

"Wipe your feet! Don't trail mud onto the nice clean floors!" Mum called. Her voice echoed against the bare walls of the empty living room.

I stepped into the hall. The house smelled of paint. The decorators had just finished on Thursday. It was hot in the house, much hotter than outside.

"This kitchen light won't go on," Dad called from the back. "Have the decorators turned off the electricity or something?"

"How should I know?" Mum shouted back.

Their voices sounded so loud in the big, empty house.

"Mum — there's someone upstairs!" I cried, wiping my feet on the new welcome mat and hurrying into the living room.

She was at the window, staring out at the rain, looking for the removal van probably. She spun round as I came in. "What?"

"There's a boy upstairs. I saw him in the

window," I said, struggling to catch my breath.

Josh entered the room from the back hall. He'd probably been with Dad. He laughed. "Is someone already living here?"

"There's no one upstairs," Mum said, rolling her eyes. "Are you two going to give me a break today, or what?"

"What did *I* do?" Josh whined.

"Listen, Amanda, we're all a little on edge today —" Mum started.

But I interrupted her. "I saw his face, Mum. In the window. I'm not crazy, you know."

"Says who?" Josh teased.

"Amanda!" Mum bit her lower lip, the way she always did when she was really exasperated. "You saw a reflection of something. Of a tree probably." She turned back to the window. The rain was coming down in sheets now, the wind driving it noisily against the large picture window.

I ran to the stairway, cupped my hands over my mouth, and shouted up to the first floor, "Who's up there?"

No answer.

"Who's up there?" I called, a little louder.

Mum had her hands over her ears. "Amanda — please!"

Josh had disappeared through the dining room. He was finally exploring the house.

"There's someone up there," I insisted and,

impulsively, I started up the wooden staircase, my trainers thudding loudly on the bare steps.

"Amanda —" I heard Mum call after me.

But I was too angry to stop. Why didn't she believe me? Why did she have to say it was a reflection of a tree I saw up there?

I was curious. I had to know who was upstairs. I had to prove Mum wrong. I had to show her I hadn't seen a stupid reflection. I suppose I can be pretty stubborn, too. Maybe it's a family trait.

The stairs squeaked and creaked under me as I climbed. I didn't feel at all scared until I reached the first-floor landing. Then I suddenly had this heavy feeling in the pit of my stomach.

I stopped, breathing hard, leaning on the banister.

Who could it be? A burglar? A bored neighbourhood kid who had broken into an empty house for a thrill?

Maybe I shouldn't be up here alone, I realized.

Maybe the boy in the window was dangerous.

"Anybody up here?" I called, my voice suddenly trembly and weak.

Still leaning against the banister, I listened.

And I could hear footsteps scampering down the hall.

No.

Not footsteps.

The rain. That's what it was. The patter of rain against the slate-tiled roof.

For some reason, the sound made me feel a little calmer. I let go of the banister and stepped into the long, narrow hallway. It was dark up here, except for a rectangle of grey light from a small window at the other end.

I took a few steps, the old wooden floorboards creaking noisily beneath me. "Anybody up here?"

Again no answer.

I stepped up to the first doorway on my left. The door was closed. The smell of fresh paint was suffocating. There was a light switch on the wall near the door. Maybe it's for the hall light, I thought. I clicked it on. But nothing happened.

"Anybody here?"

My hand was trembling as I grabbed the door knob. It felt warm in my hand. And damp.

I turned it and, taking a deep breath, pushed open the door.

I peered into the room. Grey light filtered in through the bay window. A flash of lightning made me jump back. The thunder that followed was a dull, distant roar.

Slowly, carefully, I took a step into the room. Then another.

No sign of anybody.

This was a guest bedroom. Or it could be Josh's room if he decided he liked it.

Another flash of lightning. The sky seemed to be darkening. It was pitch-black out there even though it was just after lunchtime.

I backed into the hall. The next room down was going to be mine. It also had a bay window that looked down on the front garden.

Was the boy I saw staring down at me in *my* room?

I crept down the hall, letting my hand run along the wall for some reason, and stopped outside my door, which was also closed.

Taking a deep breath, I knocked on the door. "Who's in there?" I called.

I listened.

Silence.

Then a clap of thunder, closer than the last. I froze as if I were paralyzed, holding my breath. It was so hot up here, hot and damp. And the smell of paint was making me feel dizzy.

I grabbed the doorknob. "Anybody in there?"

I started to turn the knob — when the boy crept up from behind and grabbed my shoulder.

I couldn't breathe. I couldn't cry out.

My heart seemed to stop. My chest felt as if it were about to explode.

With a desperate, terrified effort, I spun around.

"Josh!" I shrieked. "You scared me to death! I thought —"

He let go of me and took a step back. "Gotcha!" he declared, and then started to laugh, a high-pitched laugh that echoed down the long, empty hallway.

My heart was pounding hard now. My fore-head throbbed. "You're not funny," I said angrily. I shoved him against the wall. "You really scared me."

He laughed and rolled around on the floor. He's a real sicko. I tried to shove him again but missed.

Angrily, I turned away from him — just in time to see my bedroom door slowly swinging open.

I gasped in disbelief. And froze, gaping at the moving door.

Josh stopped laughing and stood up, immediately serious, his dark eyes wide with fright.

I could hear someone moving inside the room.

I could hear whispering.

Excited giggles.

"Who — who's there?" I managed to stammer in a high little voice I didn't recognize.

The door, creaking loudly, opened a bit more, then started to close.

"Who's there?" I demanded, a bit more forcefully.

Again, I could hear whispering, someone moving about.

Josh had backed up against the wall and was edging away, towards the stairs. He had an expression on his face I'd never seen before — sheer terror.

The door, creaking like a door in a haunted house film, closed a little more.

Josh was nearly at the staircase. He was staring at me, violently motioning with his hand for me to follow.

But instead, I stepped forward, grabbed the doorknob, and pushed the door open hard.

It didn't resist.

I let go of the doorknob and stood blocking the doorway. "Who's there?"

The room was empty.

35

Thunder crashed.

It took me a few seconds to realize what was making the door move. The window on the opposite wall had been left open several centimetres. The gusting wind through the open window must have been opening and closing the door. I realized that that also explained the other sounds I'd heard inside the room, the sounds I thought were whispers.

Who had left the window open? The decorators, probably.

I took a deep breath and let it out slowly, waiting for my pounding heart to settle down to normal.

Feeling a little foolish, I walked quickly to the window and pushed it shut.

"Amanda — are you all right?" Josh whispered from the hall.

I started to answer him. But then I had a better idea.

He had practically scared me to death a few minutes before. Why not give *him* a little scare? He deserved it.

So I didn't answer him.

I could hear him take a few timid steps closer to my room. "Amanda? Amanda? You okay?"

I tiptoed over to my wardrobe, pulled the door open a third of the way. Then I laid down flat on the floor, on my back, with my head and shoulders hidden inside the wardrobe and the rest of me out in the room.

"Amanda?" Josh sounded very scared.

"Ohhhhh!" I moaned loudly.

I knew when he saw me sprawled on the floor like this, he'd totally freak out!

"Amanda — what's happening?"

He was in the doorway now. He'd see me any second now, lying in the dark room, my head hidden from view, the lightning flashing impressively and the thunder cracking outside the old window.

I took a deep breath and held it to keep from giggling.

"Amanda?" he whispered. And then he must have seen me, because he uttered a loud "Huh?!" And I heard him gasp.

And then he screamed at the top of his lungs. I heard him running down the hall to the staircase, shrieking, "Mum! Dad!" And I heard his trainers thudding down the wooden stairs, with him screaming and calling all the way down.

I sniggered to myself. Then, before I could pull myself up, I felt a rough, warm tongue licking my face.

"Petey!"

He was licking my cheeks, licking my eyelids, licking me frantically, as if he were trying to revive me, or as if to let me know that everything was okay.

"Oh, Petey! Petey!" I cried, laughing and

throwing my arms around the sweet dog. "Stop! You're getting me all sticky!"

But he wouldn't stop. He kept on licking fiercely.

The poor dog is nervous, too, I thought.

"Come on, Petey, calm down," I told him, holding his panting face away with both my hands. "There's nothing to be nervous about. This new place is going to be fun. You'll see."

That night, I was smiling to myself as I fluffed up my pillow and slid into bed. I was thinking about how terrified Josh had been that afternoon, how frightened he'd looked even after I had came prancing down the stairs, perfectly okay. How angry he was that I'd fooled him.

Of course, Mum and Dad didn't think it was funny. They were both nervous and upset because the removal van had just arrived, an hour late. They forced Josh and me to call a truce. No more scaring each other.

"It's hard *not* to get scared in this creepy old place," Josh muttered. But we reluctantly agreed not to play any more jokes on each other, if we could possibly help it.

The men, complaining about the rain, started carrying in all of our furniture. Josh and I helped show them where we wanted stuff in our rooms. They dropped my chest of drawers on the stairs, but it only got a small scratch.

The furniture looked strange and small in this big house. Josh and I tried to stay out of the way while Mum and Dad worked all day, arranging things, emptying boxes, putting clothes away. Mum even managed to get the curtains hung in my room.

What a day!

Now, a little after ten o'clock, trying to get to sleep for the first time in my new room, I turned onto my side, then onto my back. Even though this was my old bed, I couldn't get comfortable.

Everything seemed so different, so wrong. The bed didn't face the same direction as in my old bedroom. The walls were bare. I hadn't had time to put up any of my posters. The room seemed so large and empty. The shadows seemed so much darker.

My back started to itch, and then I suddenly felt itchy all over. The bed's filled with bugs! I thought, sitting up. But of course that was ridiculous. It was my same old bed with clean sheets.

I forced myself to settle back down and closed my eyes. Sometimes when I can't get to sleep, I count silently by twos, picturing each number in my mind as I think it. It usually helps to clear my mind so that I can drift off to sleep.

I tried it. Burying my face in the pillow, thinking of numbers rolling past ... 4 ... 6 ... 8 ...

I yawned loudly, still wide awake at two-twenty.

I'm going to be awake forever, I thought. I'm never going to be able to sleep in this new room.

But then I must have drifted off without realizing it. I don't know how long I slept. An hour or two at the most. It was a light, uncomfortable sleep. Then something woke me. I sat straight up, startled.

Despite the heat of the room, I felt cold all over. Looking down to the end of the bed, I saw that I had kicked off the sheet and light blanket. With a groan, I reached down for them, but then froze.

I heard whispers.

Someone was whispering across the room.

"Who — who's there?" My voice was a whisper, too, tiny and frightened.

I grabbed the covers and pulled them up to my chin.

I heard more whispers. The room came into focus as my eyes adjusted to the dim light.

The curtains. The long, sheer curtains from my old room that my mother had hung that afternoon were fluttering at the window.

So. That explained the whispers. The billowing curtains must have woken me up.

A soft, grey light floated in from outside. The curtains cast moving shadows onto the foot of my bed.

Yawning, I stretched and climbed out of bed. I felt chilled all over as I crept across the wooden floor to close the window.

As I came near, the curtains stopped billowing and floated back into place. I pushed them aside and reached out to close the window.

"Oh!"

I uttered a soft cry when I realized that the window *was* closed.

But how could the curtains flutter like that with the window closed? I stood there for a while, staring out at the greys of the night. There wasn't much of a draught. The window seemed pretty airtight.

Had I imagined the curtains billowing? Were my eyes playing tricks on me?

Yawning, I hurried back through the strange shadows to my bed and pulled the covers up as high as they would go. "Amanda, stop scaring yourself," I scolded.

When I fell asleep again a few minutes later, I had the ugliest, most terrifying dream.

I dreamed that we were all dead. Mum, Dad, Josh, and me.

At first, I saw us sitting around the dinner table in the new dining room. The room was very bright, so bright I couldn't see our faces very well. They were just a bright, white blur.

But, then, slowly, slowly, everything came into focus, and I could see that beneath our hair, we had no faces. Our skin was gone, and only our grey-green skulls were left. Bits of flesh clung to my bony cheeks. There were only deep, black sockets where my eyes had been.

The four of us, all dead, sat eating in silence. Our dinner plates, I saw, were filled with small bones. A big platter in the centre of the table was piled high with grey-green bones, human-looking bones.

And then, in this dream, our disgusting meal was interrupted by a loud knocking on the door, an insistent pounding that grew louder and louder and louder. It was Kathy, my friend from back home. I could see her at our front door, pounding on it with both fists.

I wanted to go and answer the door. I wanted to run from the dining room and pull open the door and greet Kathy. I wanted to talk to Kathy. I wanted to tell her what had happened to me, to explain that I was dead and that my face had fallen away.

I wanted to see Kathy *so* badly.

But I couldn't get up from the table. I tried and tried, but I couldn't get up.

The pounding on the door grew louder and louder, until it was deafening. But I just sat there with my gruesome family, picking up bones from my dinner plate and eating them.

I woke up with a start, the horror of the dream still with me. I could still hear the pounding in my ears. I shook my head, trying to chase the dream away.

It was morning. I could tell from the blue of the sky outside the window.

"Oh, no."

The curtains. They were billowing again, flapping noisily as they blew into the room.

I sat up and stared.

The window was still closed.

"I'll take a look at the window. There must be a draught or something," Dad said at breakfast. He shovelled in another mouthful of scrambled eggs and ham.

"But, Dad — it's so weird!" I insisted, still feeling scared. "The curtains were blowing like crazy, and the window was *closed*!"

"There might be a pane missing," Dad suggested.

"Amanda's a pain!" Josh cracked. His idea of a really witty joke.

"Don't start on your sister," Mum said, putting her plate down on the table and dropping into her chair. She looked tired. Her black hair, usually carefully pulled back, was dishevelled. She tugged at the belt on her bathrobe. "Whew. I don't think I slept two hours last night."

"Neither did I," I said, sighing. "I kept thinking that boy would turn up in my room again."

"Amanda — you've really got to stop this," Mum said sharply. "Boys in your room. Curtains blowing. You have to realize that you're nervous and your imagination is working overtime."

"But, Mum —" I started.

"Maybe a ghost was behind the curtains," Josh said, teasing. He raised up his hands and made a ghostly "oooooooh" wail.

"Whoa!" Mum put a hand on Josh's shoulder. "Remember what you promised about scaring each other?"

"It's going to be hard for all of us to adjust to this place," Dad said. "You may have dreamed about the curtains blowing, Amanda. You said you had bad dreams, right?"

The terrifying nightmare flashed back into my mind. Once again I saw the big platter of bones on the table. I shivered.

"It's so damp in here," Mum said.

"A little sunshine will help dry the place out," Dad said.

I peered out of the window. The sky had turned solid grey. Trees seemed to spread darkness over our back garden. "Where's Petey?" I asked.

"Out the back," Mum replied, swallowing a mouthful of egg. "He got up early, too. Couldn't sleep, I suppose. So I let him out."

"What are we doing today?" Josh asked. He always needed to know the plan for the day. Every detail. Mainly so he could argue about it.

46

"Your father and I still have a lot of unpacking to do," Mum said, glancing to the back hallway, which was cluttered with unopened boxes. "You two can explore the neighbourhood. See what you can find out. See if there are any other kids your age around."

"In other words, you want us to get lost!" I said.

Mum and Dad both laughed. "You're very bright, Amanda."

"But I want to help unpack *my* stuff," Josh whined. I knew he'd argue with the plan, as always.

"Go and get dressed and go for a long walk," Dad said. "Take Petey with you, okay? And take a leash for him. I left one by the front stairs."

"What about our bikes? Why can't we ride our bikes?" Josh asked.

"They're buried in the back of the garage," Dad told him. "You'll never be able to get to them. Besides, you've got a flat tyre."

"If I can't ride my bike, I'm not going out," Josh insisted, crossing his arms in front of his chest.

Mum and Dad had to argue with him. Then threaten him. Finally, he agreed to go for "a short walk".

I finished my breakfast, thinking about Kathy and my other friends back at home. I wondered what the kids were like in Dark Falls. I wondered if I'd be able to find new friends, real friends.

I volunteered to do the breakfast dishes since Mum and Dad had so much work to do. The warm water felt soothing on my hands as I sponged the plates clean. I suppose maybe I'm weird. I like washing dishes.

Behind me, from somewhere in the front of the house, I could hear Josh arguing with Dad. I could just barely make out the words over the trickle of the tap water.

"Your basketball is packed in one of these boxes," Dad was saying. Then Josh said something. Then Dad said, "How should *I* know which one?" Then Josh said something. Then Dad said, "No, I don't have time to look now. Believe it or not, your basketball isn't at the top of my list."

I stacked the last dish onto the worktop to drain, and looked for a tea-towel to dry my hands. There was none in sight. I suppose they hadn't been unpacked yet.

Wiping my hands on the front of my robe, I headed for the stairs. "I'll be dressed in five minutes," I called to Josh, who was still arguing with Dad in the living room. "Then we can go out."

I started up the front stairs, and then stopped.

Above me on the landing stood a strange girl, about my age, with short black hair. She was smiling down at me, not a warm smile, not a friendly smile, but the coldest, most frightening smile I had ever seen.

A hand touched my shoulder.

I spun round.

It was Josh. "I'm not going for a walk unless I can take my basketball," he said.

"Josh — please!" I looked back up to the landing, and the girl had gone.

I felt cold all over. My legs were all trembly. I grabbed the banister.

"Dad! Come here — please!" I called.

Josh's face filled with alarm. "Hey, I didn't do anything!" he shouted.

"No — it's — it's not you," I said, and called Dad again.

"Amanda, I'm pretty busy," Dad said, appearing below at the foot of the stairs, already perspiring from uncrating living room stuff.

"Dad, I saw somebody," I told him. "Up there. A girl." I pointed.

"Amanda, please," he replied, making a face. "Stop seeing things — okay? There's no one in this house except the four of us ... and maybe a few mice."

"Mice?" Josh asked with sudden interest. "Really? Where?"

"Dad, I didn't imagine it," I said, my voice cracking. I was really hurt that he didn't believe me.

"Amanda, look up there," Dad said, gazing up to the landing. "What do you see?"

I followed his gaze. There was a pile of clothes on the landing. Mum must have just unpacked them.

"It's just clothes," Dad said impatiently. "It's not a girl. It's clothes." He rolled his eyes.

"Sorry," I said quietly. I repeated it as I started up the stairs. "Sorry."

But I didn't really feel sorry. I felt confused.

And still scared.

Was it possible that I'd thought that a pile of clothes was a smiling girl?

No. I didn't think so.

I'm not crazy. And I've got really good eyesight.

So then, what was going on?

I opened the door to my room, turned on the ceiling light, and saw the curtains billowing out in front of the bay window.

Oh, no. Not again, I thought.

I hurried over to them. This time, the window was open.

Who opened it?

Mum, I thought.

Warm, wet air blew into the room. The sky was heavy and grey. It smelled like rain.

Turning to my bed, I had another shock.

Someone had laid out an outfit for me. A pair of faded jeans and a pale blue, sleeveless T-shirt. They were spread out side by side at the foot of the bed.

Who had put them there? Mum?

I stood at the doorway and called to her. "Mum? Mum? Did you choose some clothes for me to wear today?"

I could hear her shouting something from downstairs, but I couldn't make out the words.

Calm down, Amanda, I told myself. Calm down.

Of *course* Mum put the clothes out. Of *course* Mum put them there.

From the doorway, I heard whispering in my wardrobe.

Whispering and hushed giggling behind the wardrobe door.

This was the last straw. "What's going on here?" I yelled at the top of my lungs.

I stormed over to the wardrobe and pulled open the door.

Frantically, I pushed clothes out of the way. No one in there.

Mice? I thought. Had I heard the mice that

Dad was talking about?

"I've got to get out of here," I said aloud.

The room, I realized, was driving me crazy.

No. I was driving *myself* crazy. Imagining all these weird things.

There was a logical explanation for everything. Everything.

As I pulled up my jeans and fastened them, I said the word "logical" over and over again in my mind. I said it so many times that it didn't sound like a real word any more.

Calm down, Amanda. Calm down.

I took a deep breath and held it for ten seconds.

"Boo!"

"Josh — stop it. You didn't scare me," I told him, sounding more cross than I had meant to.

"Let's get out of here," he said, staring at me from the doorway. "This place gives me the creeps."

"Huh? You, too?" I exclaimed. "What's *your* problem?"

He started to say something, then stopped. He suddenly looked embarrassed. "Forget it," he muttered.

"No, tell me," I insisted. "What were you going to say?"

He kicked at the skirting board. "I had a really creepy dream last night," he finally admitted, looking past me to the fluttering curtains at the window.

"A dream?" I remembered my horrible dream.

"Yeah. There were these two boys in my room. And they were horrible."

"What did they do?" I asked.

"I don't remember," Josh said, avoiding my eyes. "I just remember they were scary."

"And what happened?" I asked, turning to the mirror to brush my hair.

"I woke up," he said. And then added impatiently, "Come *on*. Let's go."

"Did the boys say anything to you?" I asked.

"No. I don't think so," he answered thoughtfully. "They just laughed."

"Laughed?"

"Well, giggled, sort of," Josh said. "I don't want to talk about it any more," he snapped. "Are we going for this stupid walk, or not?"

"Okay. I'm ready," I said, putting down my brush, taking one last look in the mirror. "Let's go on this stupid walk."

I followed him down the hall. As we passed the stack of clothes on the landing, I thought about the girl I had seen standing there. And I thought about the boy in the window when we'd first arrived. And the two boys Josh had seen in his dream.

I decided it proved that Josh and I were both really nervous about moving to this new place. Maybe Mum and Dad were right. We were letting our imaginations run away with us.

It had to be our imaginations. I mean, what *else* could it be?

A few seconds later, we stepped into the back garden to get Petey. He was as glad to see us as ever, leaping on us with his muddy paws, yapping excitedly, running in frantic circles through the leaves. It cheered me up just to see him.

It was hot and muggy even though the sky was grey. There was no wind at all. The heavy, old trees stood as still as statues.

We headed down the gravel drive towards the street, our trainers kicking at the dead, brown leaves, Petey running in zigzags at our sides, first in front of us, then behind. "At least Dad hasn't asked us to rake all these old leaves," Josh said.

"He will," I warned. "I don't think he's unpacked the rake yet."

Josh made a face. We stood at the kerb, looking up at our house, the two first-floor bay windows staring back at us like eyes.

The house next door, I noticed for the first time, was about the same size as ours, except it was pebble-dashed instead of brick. The curtains in the living room were drawn shut. Some of the upstairs windows were shuttered. Tall trees cast the neighbours' house in darkness, too.

"Which way?" Josh asked, tossing a stick for Petey to chase.

I pointed up the street. "The school is up that way," I said. "Let's check it out."

The road sloped uphill. Josh picked up a small tree branch from the side of the road and used it as a walking stick. Petey kept trying to chew on it while Josh walked.

We didn't see anyone on the street or in any of the front gardens as we walked. No cars passed.

I was beginning to think the whole town was deserted, until the boy stepped out from behind the low hedge.

He popped out so suddenly, both Josh and I stopped in our tracks. "Hi," he said shyly, giving us a little wave.

"Hi," Josh and I answered at the same time.

Then, before we could pull him back, Petey ran up to the boy, sniffed his trainers, and began snarling and barking. The boy stepped back and raised his hands as if he were protecting himself. He looked really frightened.

"Petey — stop!" I cried.

Josh grabbed the dog and picked him up, but he kept growling.

"He doesn't bite," I told the boy. "He doesn't usually bark, either. I'm sorry."

"That's okay," the boy said, staring at Petey, who was squirming to get out of Josh's arms. "He probably smells something on me."

"Petey, stop!" I shouted. The dog wouldn't stop squirming. "You don't want the leash — do you?"

The boy had short, wavy blond hair and very pale blue eyes. He had a funny turned-up nose that seemed out of place on his serious-looking face. He was wearing a maroon long-sleeved sweatshirt despite the mugginess of the day, and black straight-legged jeans. He had a blue baseball cap stuffed into the back pocket of his jeans.

"I'm Amanda Benson," I said. "And this is my brother Josh."

Josh hesitantly put Petey back on the ground. The dog yipped once, stared up at the boy, whimpered softly, then sat down in the road and began to scratch himself.

"I'm Ray Thurston," the boy said, stuffing his hands into his jeans pockets, still staring warily at Petey. He seemed to relax a little, though, seeing that the dog had lost interest in barking and growling at him.

I suddenly realized that Ray looked familiar.

58

Where had I seen him before? Where? I stared hard at him until I remembered.

And then I gasped in sudden fright.

Ray was the boy, the boy in my room. The boy in the window.

"You —" I stammered accusingly. "You were in our house!"

He looked confused. "Huh?"

"You were in my room — right?" I insisted.

He laughed. "I don't get it," he said. "In your room?"

Petey raised his head and gave a low growl in Ray's direction. Then he went back to his serious scratching.

"I thought I saw you," I said, beginning to feel a little doubtful. Maybe it wasn't him. Maybe....

"I haven't been in your house in a long time," Ray said, looking down warily at Petey.

"A long time?"

"Yeah. I used to live in your house," he replied.

"Huh?" Josh and I stared at him in surprise. "Our house?"

Ray nodded. "When we first moved here," he said. He picked up a flat pebble and heaved it down the street.

Petey growled, started to chase it, changed his mind, and plopped back down on the road, his stub of a tail wagging excitedly.

Heavy clouds lowered across the sky. It

seemed to grow darker. "Where do you live now?" I asked.

Ray tossed another stone, then pointed up the road.

"Did you like our house?" Josh asked Ray.

"Yeah, it was okay," Ray told him. "Nice and shady."

"You liked it?" Josh cried. "I think it's gross. It's so dark and —"

Petey interrupted. He decided to start barking at Ray again, running up till he was a few inches in front of Ray, then backing away. Ray took a few cautious steps back to the edge of the curb.

Josh pulled the leash from the pocket of his shorts. "Sorry, Petey," he said. I held the growling dog while Josh attached the leash to his collar.

"He's never done this before. Really," I said, apologizing to Ray.

The leash seemed to confuse Petey. He tugged against it, pulling Josh across the street. But at least he'd stopped barking.

"Let's do something," Josh said impatiently.

"Like what?" Ray asked, relaxing again now that Petey was on the leash.

We all thought for a while.

"Maybe we could go to your house," Josh suggested to Ray.

Ray shook his head. "No. I don't think so," he said. "Not now anyway."

"Where is everyone?" I asked, looking up and down the empty street. "It's really dead around here, huh?"

He chuckled. "Yeah. I suppose you could say that," he said. "Want to go to the playground behind the school?"

"Yeah. Okay," I agreed.

The three of us headed up the street, Ray leading the way, me walking a few feet behind him, Josh holding his tree branch in one hand, the leash in the other, Petey running this way, then that, giving Josh a really hard time.

We didn't see the gang of kids till we'd turned the corner.

There were ten or twelve of them, mostly boys but a few girls, too. They were laughing and shouting, shoving each other playfully as they came towards us down the centre of the street. Some of them, I saw, were about my age. The rest were teenagers. They were wearing jeans and dark T-shirts. One of the girls stood out because she had long, straight blonde hair and was wearing green lycra tights.

"Hey, look!" a tall boy with slicked-back black hair cried, pointing at us.

Seeing Ray, Josh, and me, they grew quiet but didn't stop moving towards us. A few of them giggled, as if they were enjoying some kind of private joke.

The three of us stopped and watched them

approach. I smiled and waited to say hi. Petey was pulling at his leash and barking his head off.

"Hi," the tall boy with the black hair said, grinning. The others thought this was very funny for some reason. They laughed. The girl in the green tights gave a short, red-haired boy a shove that almost sent him sprawling into me.

"How's it going, Ray?" a girl with short black hair asked, smiling at Ray.

"Not bad. Hi, you lot," Ray answered. He turned to Josh and me. "These are some of my friends. They're all from the neighbourhood."

"Hi," I said, feeling awkward. I wished Petey would stop barking and pulling at his leash like that. Poor Josh was having a terrible time holding onto him.

"This is George Carpenter," Ray said, pointing to the short, red-haired boy, who nodded. "And Jerry Franklin, Karen Somerset, Bill Gregory ..." He went around the circle, naming each kid. I tried to remember all the names but, of course it was impossible.

"How do you like Dark Falls?" one of the girls asked me.

"I don't really know," I told her. "It's my first day here, really. It seems nice."

Some of the kids laughed at my answer, for some reason.

"What kind of dog is that?" George Carpenter asked Josh.

Josh, holding tight to the leash handle, told him. George stared hard at Petey, studying him, as if he had never seen a dog like Petey before.

Karen Somerset, a tall, pretty girl with short blonde hair, came up to me while some of the other kids were admiring Petey. "You know, I used to live in your house," she said softly.

"What?" I wasn't sure I'd heard her correctly.

"Let's go to the playground," Ray said, interrupting.

No one responded to Ray's suggestion.

They grew quiet. Even Petey stopped barking.

Had Karen really said that she used to live in our house? I wanted to ask her, but she had stepped back into the circle of kids.

The circle.

My mouth dropped open as I realized they had formed a circle around Josh and me.

I felt a stab of fear. Was I imagining it? Was something going on?

They all suddenly looked different to me. They were smiling, but their faces were tense, watchful, as if they expected trouble.

Two of them, I noticed, were carrying baseball bats. The girl with the green tights stared at me, looking me up and down, checking me out.

No one said a word. The street was silent except for Petey, who was now whimpering softly.

I suddenly felt very afraid.

Why were they staring at us like that?

Or was my imagination running away with me again?

I turned to Ray, who was still beside me. He didn't seem at all troubled. But he didn't return my gaze.

"Hey," I said. "What's going on?" I tried to keep it light, but my voice was pretty shaky.

I looked over at Josh. He was busy soothing Petey and hadn't noticed that things had changed.

The two boys with baseball bats held them up waist high and moved forward.

I glanced around the circle, feeling the fear tighten my chest.

The circle tightened. The kids were closing in on us.

The black clouds overhead seemed to lower. The air felt heavy and damp.

Josh was fussing with Petey's collar and still didn't see what was happening. I wondered if Ray was going to say anything, if he was going to do anything to stop them. But he stayed frozen and expressionless beside me.

The circle grew smaller as the kids closed in.

I realized I'd been holding my breath. I took a deep breath and opened my mouth to cry out.

"Hey, kids — what's going on?"

It was a man's voice, calling from outside the circle.

Everyone turned to see Mr Dawes coming quickly towards us, taking long strides as he crossed the street, his open blazer flapping behind him. He had a friendly smile on his face. "What's going on?" he asked again.

He didn't seem to realize that the gang of kids had been closing in on Josh and me.

"We're heading for the playground," George Carpenter told him, twirling the bat in his hand. "You know. To play softball."

"Good idea," Mr Dawes said, pulling down his striped tie, which had blown over his shoulder. He looked up at the darkening sky. "Hope you don't get rained out."

Several of the kids had backed up. They were standing in small groups of two or three now. The circle had completely broken up.

"Is that bat for softball or hardball?" Mr Dawes asked George.

"George doesn't know," another kid replied quickly. "He's never hit anything with it!"

The kids all laughed. George playfully menaced the kid, pretending to come at him with the bat.

Mr Dawes gave a little wave and started to leave. But then he stopped, and his eyes opened wide with surprise. "Hey," he said, flashing me a friendly smile. "Josh. Amanda. I didn't see you there."

"Good morning," I muttered. I was feeling very confused. A moment ago, I'd felt terribly scared. Now everyone was laughing and kidding around.

Had I imagined that the kids were moving in on us? Ray and Josh hadn't seemed to notice anything peculiar. Was it just me and my overactive imagination?

What would have happened if Mr Dawes hadn't come along?

"How are you two getting along in the new house?" Mr Dawes asked, smoothing back his wavy blond hair.

"Okay," Josh and I answered together. Looking up at Mr Dawes, Petey began to bark and pull at the leash.

Mr Dawes put an exaggerated hurt expression on his face. "I'm crushed," he said. "Your dog still doesn't like me." He bent over Petey. "Hey, dog — lighten up."

Petey barked back angrily.

"He doesn't seem to like *anybody* today," I told Mr Dawes apologetically.

Mr Dawes stood back up and shrugged. "Can't win 'em all." He started back to his car, parked a few metres down the street. "I'm heading over to your house," he told Josh and me. "Just want to see if there's anything I can do to help your parents. Have fun, kids."

I watched him climb into his car and drive away.

"He's a nice man," Ray said.

"Yeah," I agreed. I was still feeling uncomfortable, wondering what the kids would do now that Mr Dawes had gone.

Would they form that frightening circle again?

No. Everyone started walking, heading down the road to the playground behind the school.

They were joking with each other and talking normally, and pretty much ignored Josh and me.

I was starting to feel a little silly. It was obvious that they hadn't been trying to scare Josh and me. I must have made the whole thing up in my mind.

I must have.

At least, I told myself, I hadn't screamed or made a scene. At least I hadn't made a total fool of myself.

The playground was completely empty. I guessed that most kids had stayed inside because of the threatening sky. The playground was a large, flat grassy field, surrounded on all four sides by a tall metal fence. There were swings and slides at the end nearest the school building. There were two baseball diamonds on the other end. Beyond the fence, I could see a row of tennis courts, also deserted.

Josh tied Petey to the fence, then came running over to join the rest of us. The boy named Jerry Franklin made up the teams. Ray and I were on the same team. Josh was on the other.

As our team took the field, I felt excited and a little nervous. I'm not the best softball player in the world. I can hit the ball pretty well. But in the field, I'm a complete klutz. Luckily, Jerry sent me out to right field where not many balls are hit.

The clouds began to part a little and the sky got lighter. We played two full innings. The other team was winning, eight to two. I was having fun. I had only messed up on one play. And I hit a double my first time at bat.

It was fun being with a whole new group of kids. They seemed really nice, especially the girl called Karen Somerset, who talked to me while we waited for our turn to bat. Karen had a great smile, even though she wore a brace on all her teeth, up and down. She seemed very eager to be friends.

The sun was coming out as my team started to take the field for the beginning of the third inning. Suddenly, I heard a loud, shrill whistle. I looked around until I saw that it was Jerry Franklin, blowing a silver whistle.

Everyone came running up to him. "We'd better stop," he said, looking up at the brightening sky. "We promised our parents, remember, that we'd be home for lunch."

I glanced at my watch. It was only eleven thirty. Still early.

But to my surprise, no one protested.

They all waved to each other and called out farewells, and then began to run. I couldn't believe how fast everyone left. It was as if they were racing or something.

Karen ran past me like the others, her head down, a serious expression on her pretty face.

Then she stopped suddenly and turned around. "Nice meeting you, Amanda," she called back. "We should get together sometime."

"Great!" I called to her. "Do you know where I live?"

I couldn't hear her answer very well. She nodded, and I thought she said, "Yes, I know it. I used to live in your house."

But that *couldn't* have been what she said.

Several days went by. Josh and I were getting used to our new house and our new friends.

The kids we met every day at the playground weren't exactly friends yet. They talked to Josh and me, and let us on their teams. But it was really hard to get to know them.

In my room, I kept hearing whispers late at night, and soft giggling, but I forced myself to ignore it. One night, I thought I saw a girl dressed all in white at the end of the upstairs hall. But when I walked over to investigate, there was just a pile of dirty sheets and other bedclothes against the wall.

Josh and I were adjusting, but Petey was still acting really strangely. We took him with us to the playground every day, but we had to tie him to the fence. Otherwise, he'd bark and snap at all the kids.

"He's still nervous being in a new place," I told Josh. "He'll calm down."

But Petey didn't calm down. And about two weeks later, we were finishing a softball game with Ray, and Karen Somerset, and Jerry Franklin, and George Carpenter, and a lot of other kids, when I looked over to the fence and saw that Petey had gone.

Somehow he had broken from his leash and run away.

We looked for hours, calling "Petey!" wandering from street to street, searching front gardens and back gardens, wasteground and woods. Then, after circling the neighbourhood twice, Josh and I suddenly realized we had no idea where we were.

The streets of Dark Falls all looked the same. They were all lined with sprawling old brick or pebble-dashed houses, all filled with shady old trees.

"I don't believe it. We're lost," Josh said, leaning against a tree trunk, trying to catch his breath.

"That stupid dog," I muttered, my eyes searching up the street. "Why did he do this? He's never run away before."

"I don't know how he got loose," Josh said, shaking his head, then wiping his sweaty forehead with the sleeve of his T-shirt. "I tied him up really well."

"Hey — maybe he ran home," I said. The idea immediately cheered me up.

"Yeah!" Josh stepped away from the tree and

headed back over to me. "I'll bet you're right, Amanda. He's probably been home for hours. Wow. We've been stupid. We should've checked at home first. Let's go!"

"Well," I said, looking around at the empty gardens, "we just have to work out which way is home."

I looked up and down the street, trying to decide which way we'd turned when we'd left the school playground. I couldn't remember, so we just started walking.

Luckily, as we reached the next corner, the school came into sight. We had made a full circle. It was easy to find our way from there.

Passing the playground, I stared at the spot on the fence where Petey had been tied. That troublemaking dog. He'd been behaving so badly since we came to Dark Falls.

Would he be at home when we got there? I hoped so.

A few minutes later, Josh and I were running up the gravel drive, calling the dog's name at the top of our lungs. The front door burst open and Mum, her hair tied in a red bandanna, the knees of her jeans covered with dust, leaned out. She and Dad had been painting the back porch. "Where have you two been?" Lunchtime was two hours ago!"

Josh and I both answered at the same time. "Is Petey here?"

"We've been looking for Petey!"

"Is he here?"

Mum's face filled with confusion. "Petey? I thought he was with you."

My heart sank. Josh slumped to the drive with a loud sigh, sprawling flat on his back in the gravel and leaves.

"You haven't seen him?" I asked, my trembling voice showing my disappointment. "He *was* with us. But he ran away."

"Oh. I'm sorry," Mum said, motioning for Josh to get up from the drive. "He ran away? I thought you'd been keeping him on a leash."

"You've got to help us find him," Josh pleaded, not budging from the ground. "Get the car. We've got to find him — right now!"

"I'm sure he hasn't gone far," Mum said. "You must be starving. Come in and have some lunch and then we'll —"

"No. Right *now*!" Josh screamed.

"What's going on?" Dad, his face and hair covered with tiny flecks of white paint, joined Mum on the front porch. "Josh — what's all the yelling about?"

We explained to Dad what had happened. He said he was too busy to drive around looking for Petey. Mum said she'd do it, but only after we had some lunch. I pulled Josh up by both arms and dragged him into the house.

We washed our hands and gulped down some

peanut butter and jam sandwiches. Then Mum took the car out of the garage, and we drove around and around the neighbourhood searching for our lost pet.

With no luck.

No sign of him.

Josh and I were miserable. Heartbroken. Mum and Dad called the local police. Dad kept saying that Petey had a good sense of direction, that he'd show up any minute.

But we didn't really believe it.

Where was he?

The four of us ate dinner in silence. It was the longest, most horrible evening of my life. "I tied him up really well," Josh repeated, close to tears, his dinner plate still full.

"Dogs are great escape artists," Dad said. "Don't worry. He'll show up."

"Some night for a party," Mum said glumly.

I'd competely forgotten that they were going out. Some neighbours round the corner had invited them to a big pot-luck dinner party.

"I really don't feel like partying, either," Dad said with a sigh. "I'm worn out from painting all day. But I suppose we have to be neighbourly. Are you sure you kids will be okay here?"

"Yeah, I suppose so," I said, thinking about Petey. I kept listening for his bark, listening for scratching at the door.

But no. The hours dragged by. Petey still

hadn't appeared by bedtime.

Josh and I both slipped upstairs. I felt really tired, weary from all the worrying, and the running around and searching for Petey, I suppose. But I knew I'd never be able to get to sleep.

In the hall outside my bedroom door, I heard whispering from inside my room and quiet footsteps. The usual sounds my room made. I wasn't at all scared of them or surprised by them any more.

Without hesitating, I walked into my room and clicked on the light. The room was empty, as I knew it would be. The mysterious sounds disappeared. I glanced at the curtains, which lay straight and still.

Then I saw the clothes strewn all over my bed.

Several pairs of jeans. Several T-shirts. A couple of sweatshirts. My only smart skirt.

That's strange, I thought. Mum was such a neatness freak. If she'd washed these things, surely she would have hung them up or put them into the chest of drawers.

Sighing wearily, I started to gather up the clothes and put them away. I decided that Mum simply had too much to do to be bothered. She had probably washed the stuff and then left it here for me to put away. Or she had put it all down, planning to come back later and put it away, and then got distracted with other tasks.

Half an hour later, I was tucked up in my bed wide awake, staring at the shadows on the ceiling. Some time after that — I lost track of the time — I was still wide awake, still thinking about Petey, thinking about the new kids I'd met, thinking about the neighbourhood, when I heard my bedroom door creak and swing open.

Footsteps on the creaking floorboards.

I sat up in the darkness as someone crept into my room.

"Amanda — ssshh — it's me."

Alarmed, it took me a few seconds to recognize the hushed whisper. "Josh! What do you want? What are you doing in here?"

I gasped as a blinding light forced me to cover my eyes. "Oops. Sorry," Josh said. "My torch. I didn't mean to —"

"Ow, that's bright," I said, blinking. He aimed the powerful beam of white light up at the ceiling.

"Yeah. It's a halogen torch," he said.

"Well, what do you want?" I asked irritably. I still couldn't see very well. I rubbed my eyes, but it didn't help.

"I know where Petey is," Josh whispered, "and I'm going to go and get him. Come with me?"

"Huh?" I looked at the little clock on my bedside table. "It's after midnight, Josh."

"So? It won't take long. Really."

My eyes were nearly normal by now. Staring at Josh in the light from the halogen torch, I noticed for the first time that he was fully dressed in jeans and a long-sleeved T-shirt.

"I don't get it, Josh," I said, swinging around and putting my feet on the floor. "We've looked everywhere. Where do you think Petey is?"

"In the cemetery," Josh answered. His eyes looked big and dark and serious in the white light.

"Huh?"

"That's where he ran the first time, remember? When we first came to Dark Falls? He ran to that cemetery just past the school.

"Now, wait a minute —" I started.

"We drove past it this afternoon, but we didn't look inside. He's there, Amanda. I know he is. And I'm going to get him whether you come or not."

"Josh, calm down," I said, putting my hands on his narrow shoulders. I was surprised to discover that he was trembling. "There's no reason for Petey to be in that cemetery."

"That's where he went the first time," Josh insisted. "He was looking for something there that day. I could tell. I know he's there again, Amanda." He pulled away from me. "Are you coming or not?"

My brother has to be the stubbornest, most headstrong person in the world.

"Josh, you're really going to walk into a strange cemetery so late at night?" I asked.

"I'm not afraid," he said, shining the bright light around my room.

For a brief second, I thought the light caught someone, lurking behind the curtains. I opened my mouth to cry out. But there was no one there.

"You coming or not?" he repeated impatiently.

I was going to say no. But then, glancing at the curtains, I thought, it's probably no more spooky out there in that cemetery than it is here in my own bedroom!

"Yeah. Okay," I said grudgingly. "Get out of here and let me get dressed."

"Okay," he whispered, turning off the torch, plunging us into blackness. "Meet me down at the end of the drive."

"Josh — one quick look at the cemetery, then we hurry home. Got it?" I told him.

"Yeah. Right. We'll be home before Mum and Dad get back from their party." He crept out. I could hear him making his way quickly down the stairs.

This is the craziest idea ever, I told myself as I searched in the darkness for some clothes to pull on.

And it was also sort of exciting.

Josh was wrong. No doubt about it. Petey wouldn't be hanging around in that cemetery now. Why on earth should he?

But at least it wasn't a long walk. And it was an adventure. Something to write about to Kathy back home.

And if Josh happened to be right, and we did manage to find poor, lost Petey, well, that would be great, too.

A few minutes later, dressed in jeans and a sweatshirt, I crept out of the house and joined Josh at the bottom of the drive. The night was still warm. A heavy blanket of clouds covered the moon. I realized for the first time that there were no streetlights in our road.

Josh had the halogen torch on, aimed down at our feet. "You ready?" he asked.

Stupid question. Would I be standing there if I wasn't ready?

We crunched over dead leaves as we headed up the road, towards the school. From there, it was just two blocks to the cemetery.

"It's so dark," I whispered. The houses were black and silent. There was no breeze at all. It was as if we were all alone in the world.

"It's too quiet," I said, hurrying to keep up with Josh. "No crickets or anything. Are you sure you really want to go to the cemetery?"

"I'm sure," he said, his eyes following the circle of light from the torch as it bumped over the ground. "I really think Petey is there."

We walked in the road, keeping close to the pavement. We had gone nearly two blocks. The school was just coming into sight on the next block when we heard scraping steps behind us on the pavement.

Josh and I both stopped. He lowered the light.

We both heard the sounds. I wasn't imagining them.

Someone was following us.

Josh was so startled, the torch tumbled from his hand and clattered onto the street. The light flickered but didn't go out.

By the time Josh had managed to pick it up, our pursuer had caught up with us. I spun round to face him, my heart pounding in my chest.

"Ray! What are *you* doing here?"

Josh aimed the light at Ray's face, but Ray shot his arms up to shield his face and ducked back into the darkness. "What are *you two* doing here?" he cried, sounding almost as startled as I did.

"You — you scared us," Josh said angrily, aiming the torch back down at our feet.

"Sorry," Ray said, "I would've called out, but I wasn't sure it was you."

"Josh has this crazy idea about where Petey might be," I told him, still struggling to catch my breath. "That's why we're out here."

"What about you?" Josh asked Ray.

"Well, sometimes I have trouble sleeping," Ray said softly.

"Don't your parents mind you being out so late?" I asked.

In the glow from the torch, I could see a wicked smile cross his face. "They don't know."

"Are we going to the cemetery or not?" Josh asked impatiently. Without waiting for an answer, he started jogging up the road, the light bobbing on the pavement in front of him. I turned and followed, wanting to stay close to the light.

"Where are you going?" Ray called, hurrying to catch up.

"The cemetery," I called back.

"No," Ray said. "You're not."

His voice was so low, so threatening, that I stopped. "What?"

"You're not going there," Ray repeated. I couldn't see his face. It was hidden in darkness. But his words sounded menacing.

"Hurry!" Josh called back to us. He hadn't slowed down. He didn't seem to notice the threat in Ray's words.

"Stop, Josh!" Ray called. It sounded more like an order than a request. "You can't go there!"

"Why not?" I demanded, suddenly afraid. Was Ray threatening Josh and me? Did he know something we didn't? Or was I making a big deal out of nothing again?

I stared out into the darkness, trying to see his face.

"You'd be nuts to go there at night!" he declared.

I began to think I had misjudged him. He was afraid to go there. That's why he was trying to stop us.

"Are you coming or not?" Josh demanded, getting further and further ahead of us.

"I don't think we should," Ray warned.

Yes, he's afraid, I decided. I only imagined that he was threatening us.

"You don't have to. But *we* do," Josh insisted, picking up his speed.

"No. Really," Ray said. "This is a bad idea." By now he and I were running side by side to catch up with Josh.

"Petey's there," Josh said, "I know he is."

We passed the dark, silent school. It seemed much bigger at night. Josh's light flashed through the low tree branches as we turned the corner into Cemetery Drive.

"Wait — please," Ray pleaded. But Josh didn't slow down. Neither did I. I was eager to get there and get it over with.

I wiped my forehead with my sleeve. The air was hot and still. I wished I hadn't worn long sleeves. I felt my hair. It was dripping wet.

The clouds still covered the moon as we reached the cemetery. We went through a gate in the low wall. In the darkness, I could see the crooked rows of gravestones.

Josh's light travelled from stone to stone, jumping up and down as he walked. "Petey!" he called suddenly, interrupting the silence.

He's disturbing the sleep of the dead, I thought, feeling a sudden chill of fear.

Don't be silly, Amanda. "Petey!" I called, too, forcing away my morbid thoughts.

"This is a very bad idea," Ray said, standing very close to me.

"Petey! Petey!" Josh called.

"I know it's a bad idea," I admitted to Ray. "But I didn't want Josh to come here by himself."

"But we shouldn't *be* here," Ray insisted.

I was beginning to wish he'd go away. No one had forced him to come. Why was he giving us such a hard time?

"Hey — look at this!" Josh called from several metres up ahead.

My trainers crunching over the soft ground, I hurried between the rows of graves. I hadn't realized that we had already walked the whole length of the graveyard.

"Look," Josh said again, his torch playing over a strange structure built at the edge of the cemetery.

It took me a little while to work out what it was in the small circle of light. It was so unexpected.

It was some kind of theatre. An amphitheatre, I suppose you'd call it, circular rows of bench seats dug into the ground, descending like stairs to a low stage-like platform at the bottom.

"What on earth!" I exclaimed.

I started forward to get a closer look.

"Amanda — wait. Let's go home," Ray called. He grabbed at my arm, but I hurried away, and he grabbed only air.

"Weird! Who would build an outdoor theatre at the edge of a cemetery?" I asked.

I looked back to see if Josh and Ray were following me, and my trainer caught against something. I stumbled to the ground, hitting my knee hard.

"Ow. What was that?"

Josh shone the light on it as I climbed slowly, painfully, to my feet. I had tripped over an enormous, upraised tree root.

In the flickering light, I followed the gnarled root over to a wide, old tree several metres away. The huge tree was bent over the strange below-ground theatre, leaning at such a low angle that it looked likely to topple over at any second. Big clumps of roots were raised up from the ground. Overhead, the tree's branches, heavy with leaves, seemed to lean to the ground.

"Timberrr!" Josh yelled.

"How weird!" I exclaimed. "Hey, Ray — what is this place?"

"It's a meeting place," Ray said quietly, standing close beside me, staring straight ahead at the leaning tree. "They use it sort of like a town hall. They have town meetings here."

"In the cemetery?" I cried, finding it hard to believe.

"Let's go," Ray urged, looking very nervous.

All three of us heard the footsteps. They were behind us, somewhere in the rows of graves. We turned around. Josh's light swept over the ground.

"Petey!"

There he was, standing between the nearest row of low, stone grave markers. I turned happily to Josh. "I don't believe it!" I cried. "You were right!"

"Petey! Petey!" Josh and I both started running towards our dog.

But Petey arched back on his hind legs as if he were getting ready to run away. He stared at us, his eyes red as jewels in the light of the torch.

"Petey! We've found you!" I cried.

The dog lowered his head and started to trot away.

"Petey! Hey — come back! Don't you recognize us?"

With a burst of speed, Josh caught up with him and grabbed him up off the ground. "Hey, Petey, what's the matter, fella?"

As I hurried over, Josh dropped Petey back to

87

the ground and stepped back. "Ooh — he stinks!"

"What?" I cried.

"Petey — he stinks. He smells like a dead rat!" Josh held his nose.

Petey started to walk slowly away.

"Josh, he isn't glad to see us," I wailed. "He doesn't even seem to recognize us. Look at him!"

It was true. Petey walked to the next row of gravestones, then turned and glared at us.

I suddenly felt sick. What had happened to Petey? Why was he acting so differently? Why wasn't he glad to see us?

"I don't get it," Josh said, still making a face from the odour the dog gave off. "Usually, if we leave the room for thirty seconds, he goes nuts when we come back."

"We'd better go!" Ray called. He was still at the edge of the cemetery near the leaning tree.

"Petey — what's wrong with you?" I called to the dog. He didn't respond. "Don't you remember your name? Petey? Petey?"

"Yuck! What a stink!" Josh exclaimed.

"We've got to get him home and give him a bath," I said. My voice was shaking. I felt really sad. And frightened.

"Maybe this isn't Petey," Josh said thoughtfully. The dog's eyes again glared red in the beam of light.

"It's him all right," I said quietly. "Look. He's

dragging the leash. Go and get him, Josh — and let's go home."

"*You* get him!" Josh cried. "He smells too bad!"

"Just grab his leash. You don't have to pick him up," I said.

"No. *You.*"

Josh was being stubborn again. I could see that I had no choice. "Okay," I said. "I'll get him. But I'll need the light." I grabbed the torch from Josh's hand and started to run towards Petey.

"Sit, Petey. Sit!" I ordered. It was the only command Petey ever obeyed.

But he didn't obey it this time. Instead, he turned and trotted away, holding his head down low.

"Petey — stop! Petey, come on!" I yelled, exasperated. "Don't make me chase you."

"Don't let him get away!" Josh yelled, running up behind me.

I moved the torch from side to side along the ground. "Where is he?"

"Petey! Petey!" Josh called, sounding shrill and desperate.

I couldn't see him.

"Oh, no. Don't tell me we've lost him again!" I said.

We both started to call him. "What's *wrong* with that mutt?" I cried.

I moved the beam of light down one long row

of gravestones, then, moving quickly, down the next. No sign of him. We both kept calling his name.

And then the circle of light came to rest on the front of a granite tombstone.

Reading the name on the stone, I stopped short.

And gasped.

"Josh — look!" I grabbed Josh's sleeve. I held on tight.

"Huh? What's wrong?" His face filled with confusion.

"Look! The name on the gravestone."

It was Karen Somerset.

Josh read the name. He stared at me, still confused.

"That's my new friend Karen. The one I talk to in the playground every day," I said.

"Huh? It must be her grandmother or something," Josh said, and then added impatiently, "Come on. Look for Petey."

"No. Look at the dates," I said to him.

We both read the dates under Karen Somerset's name. 1960–1972.

"It can't be her grandmother," I said, keeping the beam of light on the stone despite my trembling hand. "This girl died when she was twelve. My age. And Karen is twelve, too. She told me."

"Amanda —" Josh scowled and looked away.

But I took a few steps and beamed the light onto the next gravestone. There was a name on it I'd never heard before. I moved on to the next stone. Another name I'd never heard.

"Amanda, come on!" Josh whined.

The next gravestone had the name George Carpenter on it. 1975—1988.

"Josh — look! It's George from the playground," I called.

"Amanda, we have to get Petey," he insisted.

But I couldn't pull myself away from the gravestones. I went from one to the next, moving the torch over the engraved letters.

To my growing horror, I found Jerry Franklin. And then Bill Gregory.

All the kids we had played softball with. They all had gravestones here.

My heart thudding, I moved down the crooked row, my trainers sinking into the soft grass. I felt numb, numb with fear. I struggled to hold the light steady as I beamed it onto the last stone in the row.

RAY THURSTON. 1977—1988.

"Huh?"

I could hear Josh calling me, but I couldn't make out what he was saying.

The rest of the world seemed to fall away. I read the deeply etched inscription again:

RAY THURSTON. 1977-1988.

I stood there, staring at the letters and

numbers. I stared at them till they didn't make sense any more, until they were just a grey blur.

Suddenly, I realized that Ray had crept up beside the gravestone and was staring at me.

"Ray —" I managed to say, moving the light over the name on the stone. "Ray, this one is ... *you!*"

His eyes flared, glowing like dying embers.

"Yes, it's me," he said softly, moving towards me. "I'm so sorry, Amanda."

I took a step back, my trainers sinking into the soft ground. The air was heavy and still. No one made a sound. Nothing moved.

Dead.

I'm surrounded by death, I thought.

Then, frozen to the spot, unable to breathe, the darkness swirling around me, the gravestones spinning in their own black shadows, I thought: What is he going to do to me?

"Ray —" I managed to call out. My voice sounded faint and far away. "Ray, are you really dead?"

"I'm sorry. You weren't supposed to find out yet," he said, his voice floating low and heavy on the stifling night air.

"But — how? I mean . . . I don't understand. . . ." I looked past him to the darting white light of the torch. Josh was several rows away, almost at the road, still searching for Petey.

"Petey!" I whispered, dread choking my throat,

my stomach tightening in horror.

"Dogs always know," Ray said in a low, flat tone. "Dogs always recognize the living dead. That's why they have to go first. They always know."

"You mean — Petey's . . . dead?" I choked out the words.

Ray nodded. "They kill the dogs first."

"No!" I screamed and took another step back, nearly losing my balance as I bumped into a low marble gravestone. I jumped away from it.

"You weren't supposed to see this," Ray said, his narrow face expressionless except for his dark eyes, which revealed real sadness. "You weren't supposed to know. Not for another few weeks, anyway. I'm the watcher. I was supposed to watch, to make sure you didn't see until it was time."

He took a step towards me, his eyes lighting up red, burning into mine.

"Were you watching me from the window?" I cried. "Was that you in my room?"

Again he nodded yes. "I used to live in your house," he said, taking another step closer, forcing me back against the cold marble stone. "I'm the watcher."

I forced myself to look away, to stop staring into his glowing eyes. I wanted to scream to Josh to run and get help. But he was too far away. And I was frozen there, frozen with fear.

"We need fresh blood," Ray said.

"What?" I cried. "What are you saying?"

"The town — it can't survive without fresh blood. None of us can. You'll understand soon, Amanda. You'll understand why we had to invite you to the house, to the . . . Dead House."

In the darting, zigzagging beam of light, I could see Josh moving closer, heading our way.

Run, Josh, I thought. Run away. Fast. Get someone. Get *anyone*.

I could think the words. Why couldn't I scream them?

Ray's eyes glowed brighter. He was standing right in front of me now, his features set, hard and cold.

"Ray?" Even through my jeans, the marble gravestone felt cold against the back of my legs.

"I messed up," he whispered. "I was the watcher. But I messed up."

"Ray — what are you going to do?"

His red eyes flickered. "I'm really sorry."

He started to raise himself off the ground, to float over me.

I could feel myself start to choke. I couldn't breathe. I couldn't move. I opened my mouth to call out to Josh, but no sound came out.

Josh? Where was he?

I looked down the rows of gravestones but couldn't see his light.

Ray floated up a little higher. He hovered over

me, choking me somehow, blinding me, suffocating me.

I'm dead, I thought. Dead.

Now I'm dead, too.

And then, suddenly, light broke through the darkness.

The light shone in Ray's face, the bright white halogen light.

"What's going on?" Josh asked, in a high-pitched, nervous voice. "Amanda — what's happening?"

Ray cried out and dropped back to the ground. "Turn that off! Turn it off!" he screeched, his voice a shrill whisper, like wind through a broken windowpane.

But Josh held the bright beam of light on Ray. "What's going on? What are you doing?"

I could breathe again. As I stared into the light, I struggled to stop my heart from pounding so hard.

Ray moved his arms to shield himself from the light. But I could see what was happening to him. The light had already done its damage.

Ray's skin seemed to be melting. His whole

face sagged, then fell, dropping off his skull.

I stared into the circle of white light, unable to look away, as Ray's skin folded and drooped and melted away. As the bone underneath was revealed, his eyeballs rolled out of their sockets and fell silently to the ground.

Josh, frozen in horror, somehow held the bright light steady, and we both stared at the grinning skull, its dark craters staring back at us.

"Oh!" I shrieked as Ray took a step towards me.

But then I realized that Ray wasn't walking. He was falling.

I jumped aside as he crumpled to the ground. And gasped as his skull hit the top of the marble gravestone, and cracked open with a sickening *splat*.

"Come on!" Josh shouted. "Amanda — come *on*!" He grabbed my hand and tried to pull me away.

But I couldn't stop staring down at Ray, now a pile of bones inside a puddle of crumpled clothes.

"Amanda, come on!"

Then, before I knew it, I was running, running beside Josh as fast as I could down the long rows of graves towards the street. The light flashed against the blur of gravestones as we ran, slipping on the soft, dew-covered grass, gasping in the still, hot air.

"We've got to tell Mum and Dad. Got to get *away* from here!" I cried.

"They — they won't believe it!" Josh said, as we reached the street. We kept running, our shoes thudding hard against the pavement. "I'm not sure I believe it myself!"

"They've *got* to believe us!" I told him. "If they don't, we'll *drag* them out of that house."

The white beam of light pointed the way as we ran through the dark, silent streets. There were no streetlights, no lights on in the windows of the houses we passed, no car headlights.

Such a dark world we had entered.

And now it was time to get out.

We ran the rest of the way home. I kept looking back to see if we were being followed. But I didn't see anyone. The neighbourhood was still and empty.

I had a sharp pain in my side as we reached home. But I forced myself to keep running, up the gravel drive with its thick blanket of dead leaves, and onto the front porch.

I pushed open the door and both Josh and I started to scream. "Mum! Dad! Where are you?"

Silence.

We ran into the living room. The lights were all off.

"Mum? Dad? Are you here?"

Please be here, I thought, my heart racing, the pain in my side still sharp. Please be here.

We searched the house. They weren't at home.

"The pot-luck party," Josh suddenly remembered. Can they still be at that party?"

We were standing in the living room, both of us breathing hard. The pain in my side had let up just a bit. I had turned on all the lights, but the room still felt gloomy and menacing.

I glanced at the clock on the mantelpiece. Nearly two in the morning.

"They should be home by now," I said, my voice shaky and weak.

"Where did they go? Did they leave a number?" Josh was already on his way to the kitchen.

I followed him, turning on lights as we went. We went straight to the memo pad on the worktop where Mum and Dad always leave us notes.

Nothing. The pad was blank.

"We've *got* to find them!" Josh cried. He sounded very frightened. His wide eyes reflected his fear. "We have to get away from here."

What if something has happened to them?

That's what I started to say. But I caught myself just in time. I didn't want to scare Josh any more than he was already.

Besides, he'd probably thought of that, too.

"Should we call the police?" he asked, as we walked back to the living room and peeped out of the front window into the darkness.

"I don't know," I said, pressing my hot forehead against the cool glass. "I just don't know *what* to do. I want them to be home. I want them here so we can all leave."

"What's your hurry?" a girl's voice said from behind me.

Josh and I both cried out and spun round.

Karen Somerset was standing in the middle of the room, her arms crossed over her chest.

"But — you're *dead*!" I blurted out.

She smiled, a sad smile, a bitter smile.

And then two more kids stepped in from the hallway. One of them clicked off the lights. "Too bright in here," he said. They moved next to Karen.

And another kid, Jerry Franklin — another dead kid — appeared by the fireplace. And I saw the girl with short black hair, the one I had seen on the stairs, move next to me by the curtains.

They were all smiling, their eyes glowing dully in the dim light, all moving in on Josh and me.

"What do you *want*?" I screamed in a voice I didn't even recognize. "What are you going to do?"

"We used to live in your house," Karen said softly.

"Huh?" I cried.

"We used to live in your house," George said.

"And now, guess what?" Jerry added. "*Now we're dead in your house!*"

The others started to laugh, crackling, dry laughs, as they all closed in on Josh and me.

"They're going to kill us!" Josh cried.

I watched them move forwards in silence. Josh and I had backed up to the window. I looked around the dark room for an escape route.

But there was nowhere to run.

"Karen — you seemed so nice," I said. The words just tumbled out. I hadn't thought before I said them.

Her eyes glowed a little brighter. "I *was* nice," she said in a glum monotone, "until I moved here."

"We were all nice," George Carpenter said in the same low monotone. "But now we're dead."

"Let us go!" Josh cried, raising his hands in front of him as if to shield himself. "Please — let us go."

They laughed again, the dry, hoarse laughter. Dead laughter.

"Don't be scared, Amanda," Karen said. "Soon

you'll be with us. That's why they invited you to this house."

"Huh? I don't understand," I cried, my voice shaking.

"This is the Dead House. This is where everyone lives when they first arrive in Dark Falls. When they're still alive."

This seemed to strike the others as funny. They all sniggered and laughed.

"But our great-uncle —" Josh started.

Karen shook her head, her eyes glowing with amusement. "No. Sorry, Josh. No great-uncle. It was a trick to bring you here. Once every year, someone new has to move here. Other years, it was us. We lived in this house — until we died. This year, it's your turn."

"We need new blood," Jerry Franklin said, his eyes glowing red in the dim light. "Once a year, you see, we need new blood."

Moving forwards in silence, they hovered over Josh and me.

I took a deep breath. A last breath, perhaps. And shut my eyes.

And then I heard the knock on the door.

A loud knock, repeated several times.

I opened my eyes. The ghostly kids all vanished.

The air smelled sour.

Josh and I stared at each other, dazed, as the loud knocking started again.

"It's Mum and Dad!" Josh cried.

We both ran to the door. Josh stumbled over the coffee table in the dark, so I got to the door first.

"Mum! Dad!" I cried, pulling open the door. "Where have you been?"

I reached out my arms to hug them both — and stopped with my arms in the air. My mouth dropped open and I uttered a silent cry.

"Mr Dawes!" Josh exclaimed, coming up beside me. "We thought —"

"Oh, Mr Dawes, I'm so glad to see you!" I cried happily, pushing open the screen door for him.

"Kids — you're okay?" he asked, eyeing us both, his handsome face tight with worry. "Oh, thank God!" he cried. "I got here in time!"

"Mr Dawes —" I started, feeling so relieved, I had tears in my eyes. "I —"

He grabbed my arm. "There's no time to talk," he said, looking behind him to the street. I could see his car in the drive. The engine was running. Only the parking lights were on. "I've got to get you kids out of here while there's still time."

Josh and I started to follow him, then hesitated. What if Mr Dawes was one of them?

"Hurry," Mr Dawes urged, holding open the screen door, gazing nervously out into the darkness. "I think we're in terrible danger."

"But —" I started, staring into his frightened eyes, trying to decide if we could trust him.

"I was at the party with your parents," Mr Dawes said. "All of a sudden, they formed a circle. Everyone. Around your parents and me. They — they started to close in on us."

Just like when the kids started to close in on Josh and me, I thought.

"We broke through them and ran," Mr Dawes said, glancing to the drive behind him. "Somehow the three of us got away. Hurry. We've all got to get away from here — *now!*"

"Josh, let's go," I urged. Then I turned to Mr Dawes. "Where are Mum and Dad?"

"Come on. I'll show you. They're safe for now. But I don't know for how long."

We followed him out of the house and down the drive to his car. The clouds had parted. A sliver of moon shone low in a pale, early morning sky.

"There's something wrong with this whole town," Mr Dawes said, holding the front passenger door open for me as Josh climbed into the back.

I slumped gratefully into the seat, and he slammed the door shut. "I know," I said, as he slid behind the wheel. "Josh and I. We both— "

"We've got to get as far away as we can before they catch up with us," Mr Dawes said, backing down the drive quickly, the tyres sliding and squealing as he pulled onto the street.

"Yes," I agreed. "Thank goodness you came.

105

My house — it's filled with kids. Dead kids and —"

"So you've seen them," Mr Dawes said softly, his eyes wide with fear. He pushed down harder on the accelerator.

As I looked out into the purple darkness, a low, orange sun began to show over the green treetops. "Where are our parents?" I asked anxiously.

"There's a kind of outdoor theatre next to the cemetery," Mr Dawes said, staring straight ahead through the windscreen, his eyes narrow, his expression tense. "It's built right into the ground, and it's hidden by a big tree. I left them there. I told them not to move. I think they'll be safe. I don't think anyone'll think to look there."

"We've seen it," Josh said. A bright light suddenly flashed on in the back seat.

"What's that?" Mr Dawes asked, looking into the rear-view mirror.

"My torch," Josh answered, clicking it off. "I brought it just in case. But the sun will be up soon. I probably won't need it."

Mr Dawes hit the brake and pulled the car to the side of the road. We were at the edge of the cemetery. I climbed quickly out of the car, eager to see my parents.

The sky was still dark, streaked with violet now. The sun was a dark orange balloon just barely poking over the trees. Across the street,

106

beyond the jagged rows of gravestones, I could see the dark outline of the leaning tree that hid the mysterious amphitheatre.

"Hurry," Mr Dawes urged, closing his car door quietly. "I'm sure your parents are desperate to see you."

We headed across the street, half-walking, half-jogging, Josh swinging the torch in one hand.

Suddenly, at the edge of the cemetery grass, Josh stopped. "Petey!" he cried.

I followed his gaze, and saw our white terrier walking slowly along a slope of gravestones.

"Petey!" Josh yelled again, and began running to the dog.

My heart sank. I hadn't had a chance to tell Josh what Ray had revealed to me about Petey. "No — Josh!" I called.

Mr Dawes looked very alarmed. "We haven't got time. We've got to hurry," he said to me. Then he began shouting for Josh to come back.

"I'll go and get him," I said, and took off, running as fast as I could along the rows of graves, calling to my brother. "Josh! Josh, wait! Don't! Don't go after him! Josh — Petey's *dead*!"

Josh had been gaining on the dog, which was ambling along, sniffing the ground, not looking up, not paying any attention to Josh. Then suddenly, Josh tripped over a low gravestone.

He cried out as he fell, and the torch flew out of his hand and clattered against a gravestone.

I quickly caught up with him. "Josh — are you okay?"

He was lying on his stomach, staring straight ahead.

"Josh — answer me. Are you okay?"

I grabbed him by the shoulders and tried to pull him up, but he kept staring straight ahead, his mouth open, his eyes wide.

"Josh?"

"Look," he said finally.

I breathed a sigh of relief, knowing that Josh wasn't knocked out or anything.

"Look," he repeated, and pointed to the gravestone he had tripped over.

I turned and squinted at the grave. I read the inscription, silently mouthing the words as I read:

COMPTON DAWES. R.I.P 1950–1980.

My head began to spin. I felt dizzy. I steadied myself, holding onto Josh.

COMPTON DAWES.

It wasn't his father or his grandfather. He had told us he was the only Compton in his family.

So Mr Dawes was dead, too.

Dead. Dead. Dead.

Dead as everyone else.

He was one of them. One of the dead ones.

Josh and I stared at each other in the purple darkness. Surrounded. Surrounded by the dead.

Now what? I asked myself.

Now what?

"Get up, Josh," I said, my voice a choked whisper. "We've got to get away from here."

But we were too late.

A hand grabbed me firmly by the shoulder.

I spun round to see Mr Dawes, his eyes narrowing as he read the inscription on his own gravestone.

"Mr Dawes — you, too!" I cried, so disappointed, so confused, so . . . scared.

"Me, too," he said, almost sadly. "All of us." His eyes burned into mine. "This was a normal town once. And we were normal people. Most of us worked in the plastics factory on the outskirts of town. Then there was an accident. Something escaped from the factory. A yellow gas. It floated over the town. So fast we didn't see it . . . didn't realize. And then, it was too late, and Dark Falls wasn't a normal town any more. We were all dead, Amanda. Dead and buried. But we couldn't rest. We couldn't sleep. Dark Falls was a town of living dead."

"What — what are you going to do to us?" I managed to ask. My knees were trembling so much, I could barely stand. A dead man was squeezing my shoulder. A dead man was staring hard into my eyes.

Standing this close, I could smell his sour breath. I turned my head, but the smell was already choking my nostrils.

"Where are Mum and Dad?" Josh asked, climbing to his feet and standing rigidly opposite us, glaring accusingly at Mr Dawes.

"Safe and sound," Mr Dawes said with a faint smile. "Come with me. It's time for you to join them."

I tried to pull away from him, but his hand was locked on my shoulder. "Let go!" I shouted.

His smile grew wider. "Amanda, it doesn't hurt to die," he said softly, almost soothingly. "Come with me."

"No!" Josh shouted. And with sudden quickness, he dived to the ground and picked up his torch.

"Yes!" I cried. "Shine it on him, Josh!" The light could save us. The light could defeat Mr Dawes, as it had Ray. The light could destroy him. "Quick — shine it on him!" I pleaded.

Josh fumbled with the torch, then pointed it towards Mr Dawes's startled face, and clicked it on.

Nothing.

No light.

"It — it's broken," Josh said. "I suppose when it hit the gravestone. . . ."

My heart pounding, I looked back at Mr Dawes. The smile on his face was a smile of victory.

"Nice try," Mr Dawes said to Josh. The smile faded quickly from his face.

Close up, he didn't look so young and handsome. His skin, I could see, was dry and peeling and hung loosely beneath his eyes.

"Let's go, kids," he said, giving me a shove. He glanced up at the brightening sky. The sun was raising itself over the treetops.

Josh hesitated.

"I *said* let's go," Mr Dawes snapped impatiently. He loosened his grip on my shoulder and took a menacing step towards Josh.

Josh glanced down at the worthless torch. Then he pulled his arm back and heaved the torch at Mr Dawes's head.

The torch hit its target with a sickening *crack*. It hit Mr Dawes in the centre of his forehead, splitting a large hole in the skin.

Mr Dawes uttered a low cry. His eyes widened in surprise. Dazed, he reached a hand up to the

113

hole where a few centimetres of grey skull poked through.

"Run, Josh!" I cried.

But there was no need to tell him that. He was already zigzagging through the rows of graves, his head ducked low. I followed him, running as fast as I could.

Glancing back, I saw Mr Dawes stagger after us, still holding his ripped forehead. He took several steps, then abruptly stopped, staring up at the sky.

It's too bright for him, I realized. He has to stay in the shade.

Josh had ducked down behind a tall marble monument, old and slightly tilted, cracked down the middle. I slid down beside him, gasping for breath.

Leaning on the cool marble, we both peered around the sides of the monument. Mr Dawes, a scowl on his face, was heading back towards the amphitheatre, keeping in the shadows of the trees.

"He — he's not chasing us," Josh whispered, his chest heaving as he struggled to catch his breath and stifle his fear. "He's going back."

"The sun's too bright for him," I said, holding onto the side of the monument. "He must be going to get Mum and Dad."

"That stupid torch," Josh cried.

"Never mind that," I said, watching Mr Dawes

until he disappeared behind the big leaning tree. "What are we going to do now? I don't know —"

"Shhh. Look!" Josh poked me hard on the shoulder, and pointed. "Who's that?"

I followed his stare and saw several dark figures hurrying through the rows of tombstones. They seemed to have appeared from out of nowhere.

Had they risen out of the graves?

Walking quickly, seeming to float over the green, sloping ground, they headed into the shadows. All were walking in silence, their eyes straight ahead. They didn't stop to greet one another. They strode purposefully towards the hidden amphitheatre, as if they were being drawn there, as if they were puppets being pulled by hidden strings.

"Whoa. Look at them all!" Josh whispered, ducking his head back behind the marble monument.

The dark, moving forms made all the shadows ripple. It looked as if the trees, the gravestones, the entire cemetery had come to life, had started towards the hidden seats of the amphitheatre.

"There goes Karen," I whispered, pointing. "And George. And all the rest of them."

The kids from our house were moving quickly in twos and threes, following the other shadows, as silent and businesslike as everyone else.

Everyone was here except Ray, I thought.

Because we'd killed Ray.

We'd killed someone who was already dead.

"Do you think Mum and Dad are really down in that weird theatre?" Josh asked, interrupting my morbid thoughts, his eyes on the moving shadows.

"Come on," I said, taking Josh's hand and pulling him away from the monument. "We've got to find out."

We watched the last of the dark figures float past the enormous leaning tree. The shadows stopped moving. The cemetery was still and silent. A solitary crow floated high above in the clear blue, cloudless sky.

Slowly, Josh and I edged our way towards the amphitheatre, ducking behind gravestones, keeping low to the ground.

It was a struggle to move. I felt as if I weighed a tonne. The weight of my fear, I suppose.

I was desperate to see if Mum and Dad were there.

But at the same time, I didn't want to see.

I didn't want to see them being held prisoner by Mr Dawes and the others.

I didn't want to see them . . . killed.

The thought made me stop. I reached out an arm and halted Josh.

We were standing behind the leaning tree, hidden by its enormous clump of upraised roots. Beyond the tree, down in the theatre below, I could hear the low murmur of voices.

"Are Mum and Dad there?" Josh whispered. He started to poke his head around the side of the bent tree trunk, but I cautiously pulled him back.

"Be careful!" I whispered. "Don't let them see you. They're practically right beneath us."

"But I've *got* to know if Mum and Dad are really here," he whispered, his eyes frightened, pleading.

"Me, too," I agreed.

We both leaned over the massive trunk. The bark felt smooth under my hands as I gazed into the deep shadows cast by the tree.

And then I saw them.

Mum and Dad. They were tied up, back-to-back, standing in the centre of the floor at the bottom of the amphitheatre in front of everyone.

They looked so uncomfortable, so terrified. Their arms were tied tightly down at their sides. Dad's face was bright red. Mum's hair was all messed up, hanging wildly down over her forehead, her head bowed.

Squinting into the darkness cast by the tree, I saw Mr Dawes standing beside them along with another, older man. And I saw that the rows of long benches built into the ground were filled with people. Not a single empty space.

Everyone in town must be here, I realized.

Everyone except Josh and me.

"They're going to kill Mum and Dad," Josh

whispered, grabbing my arm, squeezing it in fear. "They're going to make Mum and Dad just like them."

"Then they'll come after us," I said, thinking out loud, staring through the shadows at my poor parents. Both of them had their heads bowed now as they stood before the silent crowd. Both of them were awaiting their fate.

"What are we going to do?" Josh whispered.

"Huh?" I was staring so hard at Mum and Dad, I suppose I momentarily blanked out.

"What are we going to do?" Josh repeated urgently, still holding on desperately to my arm. "We can't just stand here and —"

I suddenly knew what we were going to do.

It just came to me. I didn't even have to think hard.

"Maybe we can save them," I whispered, backing away from the tree. "Maybe we *can* do something."

Josh let go of my arm. He stared at me eagerly.

"We're going to push this tree over," I whispered with so much confidence that I surprised myself. "We're going to push the tree over so the sunlight will fill the amphitheatre."

"Yes!" Josh cried immediately. "Look at this tree. It's practically down already. We can do it!"

I *knew* we could do it. I don't know where my confidence came from. But I *knew* we could do it.

And I knew we had to do it fast.

Peering over the top of the trunk again, struggling to see through the shadows, I could see that everyone in the theatre had stood up. They were all starting to move forward, down towards Mum and Dad.

"Come on, Josh," I whispered. "We'll take a running jump, and push the tree over. Come on!"

Without another word, we both took several steps back.

We just had to give the trunk a good, hard push, and the tree would topple right over. The roots were already almost entirely up out of the ground, after all.

One hard push. That's all it would take. And the sunlight would pour into the theatre. Beautiful, golden sunlight. Bright, bright sunlight.

The dead people would all crumble.

And Mum and Dad would be saved.

All four of us would be saved.

"Come on, Josh," I whispered. "Ready?"

He nodded, his face solemn, his eyes frightened.

"Okay. Let's *go*!" I cried.

We both ran forward, digging our trainers into the ground, moving as fast as we could, our arms outstretched and ready.

In a second, we hit the tree trunk and pushed with all of our strength, shoving it with our hands and then moving our shoulders into it, pushing ... pushing ... pushing ...

It didn't budge.

"Push!" I cried. "Push it again!"

Josh let out an exasperated, defeated sigh. "I can't, Amanda. I can't move it."

"Josh —" I glared at him.

He backed away to try again.

Below, I could hear startled voices, angry voices.

"Quick!" I yelled. "*Push!*"

We hurtled into the tree trunk with our shoulders, both of us grunting from the effort, our muscles straining, our faces bright red.

"Push! Keep pushing!"

The veins at my temples felt about to pop.

Was the tree moving?

No.

It gave a little, but bounced right back.

The voices from below were getting louder.

"We can't do it!" I cried, so disappointed, so frustrated, so terrified. "We can't move it!"

Defeated, I slumped over onto the tree trunk,

and started to bury my face in my hands.

I pulled back with a gasp when I heard the soft cracking sound. The cracking sound grew louder until it was a rumble, then a roar. It sounded as if the ground were ripping apart.

The old tree fell quickly. It didn't have far to fall. But it fell with a thundering crash that seemed to shake the ground.

I grabbed Josh and we both stood in amazement and disbelief as bright sunlight poured into the amphitheatre.

The cries went up instantly. Horrified cries. Angry cries. Frantic cries.

The cries became howls. Howls of pain, of agony.

The people in the amphitheatre, the living dead caught in the golden light, began scrambling over one another, screeching, pulling, climbing, pushing, trying to claw their way to shade.

But it was too late.

Their skin began to drop off their bones and, as I stared open-mouthed, they crumbled to powder and dissolved to the ground, their clothes disintegrating along with them.

The painful cries continued to ring out as the bodies fell apart, the skin melted away, the dry bones collapsed. I saw Karen Somerset staggering across the floor. I saw her hair fall to the ground in a heap, revealing the dark skull underneath. She cast a glance up at me, a longing look, a look of regret. And then her eyeballs rolled out of their sockets, and she opened her toothless mouth, and she cried, "Thank you, Amanda! Thank you!" and collapsed.

Josh and I covered our ears to shut out the ghastly cries. We both looked away, unable to keep watching the entire town fall in agony and crumble to powder, destroyed by the sun, the clear, warm sun.

When we looked back, they had all disappeared.

Mum and Dad were standing right where they had been, tied back-to-back, their expressions a mixture of horror and disbelief.

"Mum! Dad!" I cried.

I'll never forget their smiles as Josh and I ran forward to free them.

It didn't take our parents long to get us packed up and to arrange for the removal men to take us back to our old neighbourhood and our old house. "I suppose it's lucky after all that we couldn't sell the old place," Dad said, as we eagerly piled into the car to leave.

Dad backed down the drive and started to roar away.

"Stop!" I cried suddenly. I'm not sure why, but I had a sudden, powerful urge to take one last look at the old house.

As both of my parents called out to me in confusion, I pushed open the door and jogged back to the drive. Standing in the middle of the garden, I stared up at the house, silent, empty, still covered in thick layers of blue-grey shadows.

I found myself gazing up at the old house as if I were hypnotized. I don't know how long I stood there.

The crunch of tyres on the gravel drive snapped me out of my spell. Startled, I turned to see a red estate car parked in the drive.

Two boys about Josh's age jumped out of the back. Their parents followed. Staring up at the house, they didn't seem to notice me.

"Here we are, kids," the mother said, smiling at them. "Our new house."

"It doesn't look new. It looks old," one of the boys said.

And then his brother's eyes widened as he noticed me. "Who are *you*?" he demanded.

The other members of his family turned to stare at me.

"Oh. I . . . uh . . ." His question caught me by surprise. I could hear my dad honking his horn impatiently down on the street. "I . . . uh . . . used to live in your house," I found myself answering.

And then I turned and ran full speed down to the street.

Wasn't that Mr Dawes standing at the porch, clipboard in hand? I wondered, catching a glimpse of a dark figure as I ran to the car.

No, it couldn't be Mr Dawes up there waiting for them, I decided.

It just couldn't be.

I didn't look back. I slammed the car door behind me, and we sped away.